Seductive NIGHTS

USA TODAY BESTSELLING AUTHOR
PJ FIALA

To the lovely women of my reader group, PJ Fiala's Road Queens, who help me out with names of characters, places, and businesses, thank you. I appreciate and adore you.

Characters
Debbie Bonsteel - Logan (Margo Price's husband)
Amy Burkhart - Anthony (Sailboat Captain)
Sharon R. Cowan - Josseline (Margo Price's youngest sister)
Marlene Davis - Addison (Margo's assistant)
Belinda Jackson Hercule - Lorraine (Thrift Store Owner) and Nathan (Logan's Lure customer)
Nancy Hoch - Jose (server at the Sandbar)
Carol Jones Karason - Marco Karason (Chef at the Sandbar)
Gayle Lazur - Crystal (Quinn's Assistant)
Karen Cranford LeBeau - Carley (Margo Price's older sister)
Elinda Moody - Krystal Jones (new server at the Sandbar)
Terra Oenning - Holly (Margo Price's younger sister)
Nicky Ortiz - Sheriff Elliott Ortiz (Miami Sheriff)
Julie Price - Margot Price (Book 3 Heroine)
Christa Stigler - Sierra Stigler (Logan Price's mistress)
Jo West - Jace Marriott (Book 3 Hero)
Dana Zamora - Gilbert Reese (Miami Sheriff's Deputy)
Debbie Zsidai - Mathias Zsidai (Miami Attorney)

Map of
Blossom Springs
Drawn by PJ Fiala

DESCRIPTION

USAT author PJ Fiala, brings you steamy, small-town romantic suspense stories, where outside forces threaten to ruin the peace and tranquility Blossom Springs was built on.

He's navigating his way through his PTSD and has found a way to thrive.

She's learning to harness her rage before it destroys everything important to her.

Together they must channel their anger and distrust towards good.

Jace Marriott learned that owning his bar and keeping his mind busy are the secrets to preventing PTSD from ruining his life. Now that he's found a sense of calm, outside forces threaten to steal it away from him.

Margo Price suffered an unimaginable loss, before being brought to her knees by an epic betrayal. Throwing herself into her real estate business is the only way she can move forward. Until she's confronted by the one person who can destroy her new found peace of mind.

Jace and Margo meet and the attraction between them burns as bright and hot as a flame. Will they end up being burned, or will their Seductive Nights together be enough to combat the evil forces set out to destroy them.

***

USA Today bestselling author PJ Fiala brings you the Servicemen of Blossom Springs series—heroes willing to sacrifice everything in service to their country, and for the men and women they love. A novel with no cliffhanger, no cheating, and a happily-ever-after guaranteed.

1

Margo trudged into the hospital room where her husband of twenty-three years, lay dying. She rotated her head, then tried rotating her shoulders, but they were stiff. She'd been in this damned hospital for nearly a week. Ever since Logan finally stopped being stubborn and went to see his doctor.

She vacillated between being pissed at Logan and being sad. She knew he'd been sick for a while, yet he refused to go to the doctor. Wasn't that just a typical man? Finally, when his pain increased to a point he couldn't tolerate, and he couldn't keep food down, he relented and went in to see his doctor. Only to be told the worst news of all.

He was dying, and he had very little time to live. As a matter of fact, he was immediately admitted into the hospital, and that's where he'd been, and she'd been since. Tests were inconclusive at this point, and she shifted between worry, fear, and irritation that in this day and age, how could a test result be inconclusive? As of this morning, he was comatose, and she knew his death was imminent. She looked across the room at her sisters, the three of them tittering and tattering quietly, and all of them froze when she walked in. If she didn't know better, she'd think their looks were guilty.

"What are you three talking about? You've had your heads together for the last day and a half. You're getting on my nerves."

Her older sister, Carley, stepped forward. "We're sorry. We know you're stressed right now, and we're not trying to add to your stress. We're just trying to figure out some of the arrangements. Wondering if you're finally in the right mind to talk about that."

Margo let out a deep breath and turned her head to stare at her husband, Logan. He hadn't moved in hours. He was frail. The color of his skin was gray. She knew the end was near. She knew him well. Her entire adult life they'd been married. They'd started Price Real Estate Company more than 15 years ago, and they'd made it a huge fucking success, and now she was going to have to run the whole thing herself. Not to mention all the things. The house. The business. And she didn't know how she'd do it without her partner in crime. They'd done everything together over the years. When they'd made a conscious decision not to have children, that decision was made based on their desire to travel. The real estate business offered them the life they'd dreamed of. Success offered them travel to exotic locations.

Carley put her arm around Margo's shoulders and squeezed her. "Margo honey, can we at least talk about a few things with the service? And don't you think you should call your pastor and have him come in to give him last rites?"

Margo swallowed the dry, hard knot that just materialized in her throat at the thought of having to watch as her husband was given last rites.

Finally, she responded softly, "Yes, please call my pastor.

And yes, we should make some arrangements. Nothing big and ostentatious. Friends and family. A small gathering in the church basement after the service. He would have wanted it that way. He was so private about so many things. I don't want to take that away from him at a time when his wishes should be honored the most."

Margo's youngest sister, Josseline, scoffed. Margo's eyes landed on hers. "Are you saying he wasn't private?"

Josseline's cheeks turned pink, her lips thinned, and her jaw tightened. "Oh, he was private, all right."

Margo raised her eyebrows. "And what does that mean?"

Her younger sister, the sister in between her and Josseline, Holly, nudged Josseline. Holly shrugged, "Nothing. It's just been a stressful time for all of us, and we just hate seeing you so sad."

Josseline nodded slowly, and Margo stared at her sisters one at a time. They'd been here for her. Gosh, they'd been her best friends her whole life. She didn't need outside friends she had these women, and they were fantastic, fabulous, loving, beautiful, smart women. She had the immense pleasure of being related to them. That was a bonus not every person got in life.

Josseline excused herself. "I'll go call the pastor."

As she walked by, she grabbed Margo's hand and squeezed. "I love you, Margo."

"I love you too, Josseline."

Her sister moved past her and out the door.

Margo stepped to the side of Logan's bed and took his hand in hers. It was cooler than it had been earlier. The time was certainly near, that was a fact. Some chiming and pinging was heard from across the room, and her sister Carley said, "I'm sorry. I forgot to turn my phone off. I'll step outside and see who needs my attention, then turn it off.

She moved quickly through the door before Margo could say anything to her. It was fine if she had her phone on. Their lives didn't stop because Logan's was about to, right?

Her shoulders slumped. How would she navigate all of this? Did she go on with her business and her life as if she'd never had Logan all these years? How did one do that?

A few moments later, a nurse entered the room. The first thing she did was touch Logan's forehead. She listened with her stethoscope to his breathing, which was so faint it was hard to hear. She typed something into her handheld computer, which looked like a bulky phone. When she finished, she glanced at Margo and smiled softly. "Is there anything you need, Margo?"

"No." She took a deep breath, "I mean, do you know how...? I mean," she watched Logan for a moment, afraid to say the next words.

She lowered her voice and whispered, "Do you know how much longer?"

The nurse shook her head slowly, her lips turned down in a frown. "I'm afraid we don't, but I can tell you it'll be imminent. I've just texted the doctor and asked him to come up here one last time."

A tear dripped down Margo's cheek and her sister Holly stepped forward and hugged her. "I'm so sorry, Margo. I'm so sorry."

At that moment Logan took a deep breath, and all Margo could do was stare.

2

Jace Marriott stood on Sunset Beach Road in front of his bar. He stared at the bar, then turned his head to the right and stared at the thrift shop next door. It was an older building made of cinder block, painted faded fuchsia, though that was peeling. It looked in need of repair, but he just found out it was going up for sale, and he wanted it. He wanted that old, dilapidated building torn down, and he wanted to expand Sarge's Sandbar. The bar he'd grown immeasurably over the last year. He wanted it to grow even further. Not so big that it would be a big giant bar with no personality. What he really wanted was to expand the inside a bit more, so he had more kitchen space. His food business was growing by leaps and bounds. He wanted the bar area to be expanded. And he'd just been informed the town council expected him to have a buffer of 30 feet all around his business as a noise barrier. He'd offered to plant trees around the area as a buffer. They said they'd take it under advisement. That meant he needed the thrift shop because, right now, he was encroaching on that buffer. He wasn't sure what he was going to do if he couldn't get the thrift shop and he couldn't plant trees. That was going to be his next big challenge.

He strode toward the front door as a truck approached. He turned to see his friend, Quinn, driving toward him. Quinn waved as he passed, then pulled into the parking area at the Sandbar and Jace hustled to meet him.

Quinn stepped out of his truck and chuckled. "What are you doing staring at the bar from the road? I almost hit you."

Jace shrugged. "I just found out that ugly old thrift shop is going up for sale and I want it."

Quinn nodded. "I was just coming to tell you that I heard that this morning when I was in the bakery. Hanna had a group of ladies, her Tuesday Ladies, as she calls them, in the bakery having a chat. They were talking about Lorraine, the owner of the Thrift Shop, moving out of town. Apparently, one of the women is friends with her. She did say she's a motivated seller."

Jace nodded. "Well, that's good to hear because I'm a motivated buyer. I'm going to need to buy that property. The town council just told me I don't have enough of a buffer between these two buildings, and I'm going to have to do something about that. Plus, I need to expand."

Quinn nodded as they walked into the bar. Quinn perched himself on a bar stool. Jace strode around behind the bar.

Quinn responded, "I heard Margot Price is listing the property from Price Realty. Do you know her?"

"I know of her. I've seen her around town here or there, and she's been here, but I don't really know her. Is that who helped you buy the barracks?"

Quinn chuckled, "One and the same. She's a very good real estate agent. I'm sure if you make a fair offer, she'll do what she can to help you buy the building."

"That's what I need. Perfect. I think I heard her husband was sick or something though, right?"

Quinn nodded. "Sounds that way. Sounds like he's not doing well. He hadn't been feeling well for a while but refused to go to the doctor. She finally made him. Sounds like he hasn't come out of the hospital since then."

Jace shook his head. "Man, life is fragile right?"

"That's a fact," Quinn responded.

Jace tapped the top of the bar. "Are you drinking something?"

Quinn looked at his watch. "Well since it's only ten in the morning I better stick to coffee. How about coffee?"

Jace shook his head. "I had to put a new coffee pot into the kitchen just for all the people coming in early in the day wanting coffee. Let me get it for you."

Jace hustled back to the kitchen, poured Quinn a cup of coffee, grabbed the creamer and sugar, and hustled back out to the bar. Setting the steaming drink in front of his friend, he asked, "How're the barracks coming anyway?"

Quinn poured creamer in his coffee and nodded. "It's coming along great. We've got the walls torn down in the first building. The architect was there yesterday. He's given us the go-ahead, and Jared's there right now getting the framing up. I'm on my way over there, but I just heard the news about the thrift shop and wanted to let you know."

"If I get this thrift shop and expand, I'm going to need to hire a couple more people, and maybe they'll be your first tenants."

Quinn nodded. "That would be good. Hopefully, I'll be ready in time. So tell me your plan with the bar. I thought you didn't want it to be this big monstrosity of a business."

"I don't, but we're bumping into each other in the kitchen, and as you know, I was retrofitting things back there as our menu grew, but now we've outgrown the kitchen, so I need more space back there. And I'm going to need some new equipment. Also, with us having music now on weekends, our business is booming, so that's making the town council a little irritated. Apparently, one of the town council members lives close enough that, get this, he thinks he heard music the other night." Jace held the first two fingers of each hand up and bent the fingers, simulating air quotes. "He thinks he heard music."

Quinn laughed. "Oh my god. Well, I'm happy to go to the next town council meeting with you if you need someone who thinks they don't hear music. I'm not that far from here, and I think I know who you're referring to. I live closer than he does."

Jace laughed. "Well, I may take you up on that. We'll see."

Quinn sipped his coffee.

Jace stared out the window a moment. "Have you set a wedding date yet?"

Quinn's grin spread to a huge smile. "We have. That's the second reason I'm here. We'd like to follow in Sid and Grace's footsteps and get married here. Maybe we won't use the stage. Hanna would kind of like the water to be a backdrop. What do you think of that?"

"Well I'm never gonna turn down business, so I think that sounds pretty fucking great."

"Good." Quinn laughed. "And I'd like you to be my best man."

Jace smiled. "I'm honored. What about Sid?"

"He's gonna be my best man too. I'm gonna have two best men."

Jace laughed. "Boy, oh boy, you two. I think that sounds pretty great. I wouldn't want Sid to be left out at all. He's good people."

"That he is. Okay, so we're getting married at the end of the month, and we're gonna have it here."

"Excellent. So are you here to make plans?"

Quinn started laughing and held his hands out in front of him. "Oh no, I wouldn't dare. I'm gonna let Hanna come in and talk to you about all that. I just told her I'd see if you had the date open here before we moved any further."

Jace grabbed his appointment book and flipped it to the end of the month. "What's the date?"

They looked over the book together. Quinn pointed to the last Thursday of the month.

"You want to get married on a Thursday?" Jace asked.

"Well, I believe you have live music here on Fridays and Saturdays, so yes, we're thinking Thursday."

"Okay, but a lot of people work during the day and aren't gonna be able to make it, so why don't you think about Sunday afternoon?"

Quinn's lips pursed a moment. "Okay, let me ask Hanna about Sunday afternoon. In the meantime, why don't you put those two days on your calendar, and I'll let you know when you can clear one of them?"

Jace chuckled. He marked Quinn and Hanna on both Thursday and Sunday and set his pencil down. "Okay, I'm going to call Margo Price's office and see about getting an offer made, and then why don't you hop skip over to Margo Price's office and tell her that your good friend, Jace Marriott, is eager to make an offer on that thrift shop, in case she doesn't know who I am."

Quinn laughed. "Oh, I think everybody knows who you are, but I'll absolutely do that for you. Let me just finish my coffee."

3

———

Margo woke and glanced at the clock on the bedside table. Six o'clock in the morning. She'd slept four hours. They'd gotten home late last night after Logan's passing. They had a glass of wine to take the edge off, and she climbed into bed exhausted at two. Her sisters were in the spare bedrooms, hopefully getting some much-needed rest. She stared at the ceiling, thinking about all that had to be done. Logan would never be here again.

Though truth be told, in recent years, he'd been away more than he'd been home. He fancied himself as a real estate agent for the entire state. He was flying down to Miami often and sometimes then up to Tallahassee brokering deals. Though he hadn't gained many new listings, he was trying. She admired him for that.

Giving herself a couple more minutes, she sat upright, rubbed her fingers around her eyes, and took a deep breath before standing.

Slowly making her way to the door, she straightened the pajamas she wore. The tank top and shorts had been a gift from Logan last year. Before opening the door and letting the day begin, she took a deep breath to steady her emotions. She silently padded down the hallway. The house was quiet right now. Her sisters, who needed as much sleep as she did, were thankfully still sleeping.

Grateful that, out of habit, she'd put the coffee pot timer on and that it was now fully brewed, she made herself a cup of coffee and decided to sit outside on the deck. It was warm already this morning. The thermometer said it was seventy. It was going to be a hot one today, near ninety-seven, if the weatherman was correct.

Silently sliding the patio door open, she stepped outside and braced herself for the humidity that hit her full force. She sat in her favorite chair, one of the teal Adirondack chairs facing her flowerbeds. Logan's favorite had been the orange chair to her right. Sipping her coffee, she absently watched the butterflies gracefully landing on the flowers.

Her mind only allowed her a few moments of tranquility before the barrage of appointments hit. They had an appointment at the funeral home today to make arrangements. She'd probably need to go to the bank and figure out what had to be done with the business accounts. Maybe that could wait until next week. Grateful that her home was paid for and she paid the bills regularly as opposed to Logan, she knew things here would be fine. Lonely, probably, but financially, she was fine. She took another sip of her coffee when she heard the patio door slide open slowly. Turning her head, she saw her oldest sister, Carley, standing in the doorway.

"Just checking to see if you had a cup of coffee. I'll bring mine out in a minute."

Margo nodded, took another sip from her cup, and waited. Carley stepped out of the house, and the cool air from the air conditioner swept out and touched her before the door closed. Carley sat in the chair next to her. Logan's chair.

"Did you sleep?" Carly asked.

"Not much. Four hours I'm guessing. How about you?"

Carley shrugged. "About the same."

She nodded her head. "I was just thinking about all the things we're going to have to do today."

"Yeah, that's what woke me up too."

"Never dreamed I'd be in this situation. At least not when I was only 43."

"Well, I guess we never know, right?"

"Right? Guess we never do."

Carley took another sip, opened her mouth to say something, and then thought better of it and closed her mouth.

Margo waited. She wasn't sure if she could handle anything else right now anyway.

Soon, her youngest sister, Josseline, stepped outside, pulled another of the teal chairs from across the deck, and sat down on the other side of Carley. She sipped her coffee, ran her hands through her long, dark hair, and let out a deep breath.

Margo glanced at her youngest sister. Her demeanor seemed off. They'd had family members pass before, and she'd never behaved like this.

"What's going on with you, Josseline?"

Her sister turned her head to stare at her. Her eyebrows shot up in her hairline. "What do you mean what's going on?"

"I mean, what's going on? Yesterday I got the feeling you were irritated about being at the hospital. Today you seem... I don't know, put out."

Josseline shook her head. "I'm not put out. We all handle

stress differently, Margo. I know that you've got a lot on your plate right now, and you don't even know what I've got on mine. So what do you want? You want me to be crying and sobbing and wailing?"

Margo's shoulders tensed. "No, I don't want that."

Her sister Carley leaned over and patted her hand. "Let's not argue. We need each other right now more than ever."

"I know." Margo let out a deep breath, took another sip of her coffee, and continued to stare at her flowers. A bee buzzed from flower to flower. She watched it for a few moments, mesmerized by the beauty of it all. The birds and the bees. It seemed so simple.

She stared at her purple cone flowers and the bee that was even now pollinating them. And she thought of Logan. Those were his favorites. A thought popped into her head.

" I think I'm gonna cut some of those purple cone flowers and take them to the flower shop and have them make an arrangement for Logan's casket. Those were his favorite flowers, and I think it's poignant that they would be coming from our garden."

Carley nodded and softly said, "That's a good idea, Margo."

Josseline said nothing, which irritated Margo, but she redirected her thoughts around how many flowers she would need to cut and how soon she would need to get them to the flower shop after she cut them. Then her thoughts jumped to what time their appointment was at the funeral home, and quite frankly, all the things began to once again circle around in her head.

Her younger sister, Holly, stepped out on the deck. Cup of coffee in hand and the coffee pot in the other to refill anyone who needed one. Without saying a word, she just went from sister to sister and refilled their cups. She stepped back inside, returned quickly, pulled up a chair, and sat on the other side of Margo. "Did you sleep, Margo?"

"About four hours I guess."

"Okay, well, that's better than three hours, right?"

Margo chuckled, "Right?"

Holly continued. "Okay, so what I was thinking is today we have to be at the funeral home at 10. Have you decided on cremation or burial?"

Margo closed her eyes for a moment. No, she hadn't decided on that at all. She let out a deep breath. "Logan had told me he wanted to be cremated." Margo tilted her head to the left. "It was weird and sudden. Out of the blue, after he was admitted, he told me to cremate him."

"Okay, well, that's good, I guess. Then we'll tell the funeral home that, and then I think we have the option of having a funeral with him right away with a viewing, and then they cremate him later, or I think it takes a week or two for the cremation and then we can have a memorial service with his ashes present. Do you know what you want?"

She let out a deep breath. "No, I don't know, but I think because we are so well known in town, we should probably have a traditional showing and then cremation. I couldn't bear to sit around for a week or two waiting for him to be cremated before going through a memorial service. At this point, I feel exhausted, and I just want to get it over with." She took a deep breath. "Does that sound harsh?"

Carley shook her head. "It doesn't sound harsh. At this point, you have to do what you think is right and what's right for you. Logan isn't here for any of it."

Josseline said nothing. She lifted her cup to her lips and sipped her coffee.

Margo sipped some more and then stood. Josseline's attitude was really getting on her nerves, and she didn't need to be arguing with her sisters right now. They were her support system.

"I'm gonna go take a shower and get dressed, and then we can eat some breakfast, and from there, we'll start the day. Will you all be with me today, or are some of you staying back?" She purposely looked at Josseline, who smiled sweetly and said, "We'll all be with you today, Margo."

She nodded once and stepped through the kitchen door. The cool air felt chilling but so welcome. She set her nearly empty cup of coffee on the counter and made her way down the hallway to her bedroom.

As soon as she entered, she stared across the room at Logan's closet. They had separate closets. When they'd built this house, that was a must. Each of them had to have their own closet. And she thought now about having to clean that out. What does one do with all of his clothes and belongings? His golf clubs, his baseball glove, his baseball bats, and his stupid hobby of making fishing bobbers and lures. God, she hated the time he spent down in the basement making his stupid fishing stuff. But it was something he loved. And then, in the last few years, when he had gotten it in his head to be THE real estate agent in Florida and started doing more traveling, his fishing bobber and lure business sort of sat in decline. Not that he'd had a strong business, but he had a few area fishermen who paid for most of the supplies he needed for his hobby. Maybe one of them would want to take over. She'd have to see if she could find their names.

She started the water in her shower and pulled her clothes from her closet. What was appropriate? Did she have to wear all black? They didn't really do that anymore, did they? She certainly wasn't living in a time where they had to wear black for a year afterward. She'd wear black at the funeral. Letting out a deeply held breath, she opted for subdued.

Stepping into the warm spray of water, she closed her eyes and let the water clean away all of the ickiness from the past few days. She sent up a prayer that this could be a cleansing of sorts. A fresh start. Afterward, she dried her hair and wondered if she should get it cut. It hung down to her bra strap. She'd always left it long because Logan loved it. But damn, it was hot in Florida. There were so many days when she thought about just chopping it off but then reasoned out that at least with it long, she could pull it up easily.

She dried her hair and dressed. She'd decided on a light pair of gray slacks and a gray and white lightweight top to match. She strode out to the kitchen and heard her sisters cooking and laughing. And tears stung her eyes. Her sister Holly saw her first and said, "Oh, Margo, we're sorry we didn't mean to make you cry."

Margo shook her head, "I'm not crying because of you all. I'm crying because the laughter sounded so good, and it feels like it's been ages since I've heard laughter in this house."

Her sisters looked at each other, their faces tense.

Carley moved to her and wrapped her arms around Margo's shoulders.

"Come on, sit down here, let us feed you. Then we'll all get ready to go and make the arrangements we need to make today." She sat and ate, though she moved her food around on her plate more than anything. But Holly had made them a wonderful omelet and some toast, and it was delicious, but she just really didn't have an appetite right now. She ate what she could.

Josseline got up and began picking up the dishes. Her

eyes landed on Margo's. "We're going have to start making phone calls. Do you want to divvy up a list of people for us to call? We can do that today so it's not a shock when they see the obituary. And speaking of, we're going to need to write an obituary."

She hadn't thought of that. She hadn't thought of any of that. "Yes..." she halted a moment, "I will..." She pulled her phone off the table and started naming off some people who had to be called. Her sisters pulled their phones out as well, and if they had that contact in their phones, they volun- teered to call that person. And then she gasped, "Oh my god, I didn't even think of this. Where's Logan's phone? I must have left it at the hospital. There'll be contacts in his phone that I don't have. I should... I should get that. Let me call the hospital."

Carley stopped her with a hand covering her hand. "No, honey, we'll take care of that okay? We'll take care of that. You take care of calling those you want to call. Go in the office, make yourself comfortable where you're alone, and make your calls. We'll make our calls out here."

"Okay." She gratefully did as she was told because right now, it felt so good to be told what needed to be done. She strolled to the office and sat down to make her first call to their receptionist, Addison, at the real estate office.

Their parents had died a few years ago, about a year apart, so she didn't have parents to call, but they did have aunts, uncles, and cousins. The sisters had all spoken to their significant others last night. So today, it was extended family and friends. Logan's parents had passed several years ago, and he was an only child, but he did have a couple of aunts and uncles she'd call. She made her calls and then made a mental note to ask for Logan's phone later on, and then she would go through his list of contacts and see who else needed to be notified.

Soon her sister Josseline tapped on the door of the office. "Hey Margo, we have to get going now. Our appointment at the funeral home is in 15 minutes."

"Oh my gosh, I didn't even realize how quickly the time passed today."

"Okay." Josseline waited for her at the door, and as soon as Margo approached, she put her arms around Margo and gave her a hug. "I'm sorry if I stressed you out. I sure don't mean to. I love you."

"I love you too, Josseline. I love you too."

Josseline sniffed lightly. "Okay, so let's get going. Grab your purse, and we'll take off."

4

Margo and her sisters finished making the arrangements. They stopped at the flower shop to deliver the purple coneflowers, and the people there said they would make Logan a beautiful arrangement for his casket. At the funeral home, she had to answer all sorts of questions. What song did she want to be played at the funeral? What verse did she want spoken? Who were the pallbearers? Oh my god, pallbearers. She never even thought of that. In the end, she opted for no pallbearers because there wasn't going to be a funeral procession. Logan's casket would be at the front of the church, their little local non-denominational church. They'd both preferred that when they first married. And in the end, he would be left there for the funeral home to take him to be cremated. She wouldn't know who to pick anyway. And, finally, the funeral would be tomorrow. Quick. Easy, as if they ever were, but her sisters talked her into not waiting since there was little need and no out-of-town relatives to wait for. It was all so surreal.

They went home, and she crashed almost immediately

and slept for 13 hours. Her body and mind finally agreed to let her sleep. When she woke, it was 5 a.m. As she stared at the ceiling for a moment, she felt rested. She got up, stretched, and ambled out to the kitchen to see Carley sitting at the table with a phone in her hand. As soon as she entered the kitchen, Carley set the phone down and smiled at her. "Did you sleep well? You must have been exhausted."

"I did. I slept very well actually. Thank you all for just occupying yourselves while you're here."

Carley shook her head. "No, no, don't worry about us. We're fine. We played a couple of friendly games of cards last night, and then we went to bed early. I think we all needed the rest."

"Yes, that's a fact. Have you decided what you'll wear for the funeral?"

Margo shushed. "I don't know. I have an older black tank dress; it's certainly in good shape. I have black slacks, but it's so ungodly hot out."

"It is. You should wear that black tank dress. It looks good on you. The dress will be cooler than slacks, and let's face it, everyone at the funeral home in the church will be as hot as you are, so I don't think you'll offend anyone. And if you do, who the fuck cares?"

Margo laughed. Carley's blunt response was out of character and so needed.

"That's exactly right. Who the fuck cares? I'll wear what I want to wear, and for the record, Logan loved that dress. He's actually the one who bought it for me when we went to Italy last year."

Carley smiled. Margo sat at the table with her sister and noticed the phone was gone. "Oh, honey, don't let me stop what you were doing with your phone. If you're in the middle of a conversation, please go ahead. I won't be offended."

"No, it's alright. I was just messing around on social media. It doesn't matter."

Her other two sisters shuffled in one by one. They sat at the table, drank their coffee, and chatted. It was nice. Margo took a deep breath. "So, did anybody think to get Logan's phone? I don't know if there are people we should have contacted about today or not."

Carley looked at her sister, placed her hand over hers, and squeezed. "We did, honey. We took care of it."

"Do you mind if I have his phone?"

Holly shrugged, "Why don't we wait till after the funeral? You may want to wait."

"No, actually, I don't want to wait. I would like Logan's phone, please."

Josseline stood quickly. "Why don't we wait, Margo? Let's go over what has to happen today and what you need help with in the real estate office?"

"No. I don't need help. We have a receptionist-personal assistant there, and she has everything completely under control. She's gathering Logan's files right now so that I can look at them first thing tomorrow when I go into the office. What I really want is Logan's phone."

Carley squeezed her hand. "No, you don't, honey. No, you don't."

Her heart beat rapidly, and she felt something sour in her stomach. "What does that mean? What are you hiding from me? You've all been acting weird. What is going on, and why can't I have my husband's phone?" Her voice rose, and she immediately regretted it when she saw them grimace.

"You can have it," Carley said, "But let's wait till later today."

"Okay, why?"

Holly leaned forward and softly replied. "It's just best if you wait. We don't want you to be upset or overly sad today."

"Overly sad? My husband of twenty-three years died. I'm going to be overly sad no matter what you think."

Holly's eyes darted to Carley's immediately.

Finally, Josseline spoke up. "Give her the phone."

"No," Carley bit back.

"Give her the phone," Josseline growled.

"No Josseline, not now."

Margo slapped her hands on top of the table. "Give me the fucking phone."

Her sisters stared at each other for a moment, and then finally, Carley turned slightly so they were face to face. Her voice softened. "Margo, you're going to find some upsetting things on Logan's phone."

"Like what?"

"We really wanted to wait till after the funeral for all of this." Carley took a deep breath and glanced at her sisters, who stared mutely.

"Logan's been having an affair."

Swirls and paisley shapes floated before her eyes. Her heart beat so fast she thought she was going to pass out. Her vision dimmed. She couldn't believe what she was hearing. Why would her sisters say this about Logan? Why would they say this?

She finally found her voice. "I can't believe that you're accusing him of having an affair at a time like this. At a time when he can't defend himself. At a time when I am griev-ing." Her voice broke.

"We tried to spare you," Carley reminded her.

"Who? Who was he having an affair with then?"

Carley let out a deep breath and looked at her sisters for help. Neither of them chimed in. She shook her head slightly, "A woman named Sierra Stigler, and they've been having an affair for about seven years. I found out because his phone kept chiming when you had left to take a walk the other day, and I looked at his phone and saw her messaging him, asking what was going on. She asked what the doctor said and if he would please respond. She was so worried. I started looking back at all the texts, and they've been communicating for seven years."

Seven years. She couldn't even talk. She opened her mouth to say something, but nothing would come out. This was the most bizarre information she'd ever gotten. Ever. And she wanted so badly to go scream at Logan and ask him what the fuck.

Carley slid the phone she had been holding before across the table. "You don't have to read this now, Margo. You can wait. You have a funeral to get through. But we're here if you want to read some of it now."

She looked at the phone like it was something that would reach out and bite her. She hated to think about what was on that phone, and then again, part of her needed to know. They wouldn't lie about something like this, would they? They loved her. They wouldn't hurt her unnecessarily. They must know something that she didn't know. They must.

Slowly, as if she were afraid of that phone, she reached forward and pulled the phone toward her. She picked it off the table and entered Logan's birth date. That had always been his password, but it didn't work.

She tried again and it still didn't work.

Carley cleared her throat lightly, "He changed it. Then I changed it to one, two, three, four, as soon as I was able to get in using his fingerprint.

Margo swallowed and entered one, two, three, four, and scrolled through his messages. The very first one on top was Sierra Stigler. Actually, it just said Sierra with a heart by it, and she wanted to burst out crying. She took a deep breath, tapped Sierra's name, and began reading the love texts. The pictures from Miami. He wasn't trying to find business in Miami. He was with his fucking mistress. Or maybe she should say he was fucking his mistress in Miami. There were pictures in Tallahassee. There were pictures in some areas she didn't know.

She started looking at the dates and then pulled her phone over and compared the same dates. The dates he told her he was fishing with the guys, and he was going off to meet a new client, and he was talking to some of the fishermen about a new fishing hole, and he had a golf outing, and he had this, and he had that, and every single lie he'd ever told her was there for her to see. And every single time he was with her. A tall, slender redhead with blue eyes, fake boobs, and Logan.

She scrolled back until she couldn't take it anymore, and she set the phone down. She stared straight ahead for what felt like an hour. Her sisters were quiet. They didn't say anything. They let her process what she needed to process. She finally took a deep breath and said, "Well, I have to go through with the funeral today because he was so well-known, and I sure as hell don't want this to ruin our business. I mean my business. After all, I need it to survive now. But I'll tell you what I'm not gonna do. I'm not gonna pick up his fucking ashes from the funeral home when they call to tell me that he's finished, and I am NOT going to erect any kind of a statue, or any kind of a memorial for that man because really now our last seven years have been nothing but a lie."

5

Jace's phone rang, and he pulled it from his pocket. The readout said Price Realty, and he huffed out a breath. He'd called two days ago and hadn't received a return phone call yet. He was worried the building next door was already sold.

"Hello, this is Jace Marriott."

"Hello, Jace. This is Margo Price. I apologize for the delay in my return phone call to you. I hope you're still interested in the thrift shop next door. That's why I'm calling."

"Yes, it's -- I am. I'm still interested. As a matter of fact, I'd like to place an offer right away."

"Don't you want to see it first?"

"Oh, absolutely, I want to see it. We can take a look, but I'm going to tear it down, so honestly, the inside means very little to me."

A brief silence fell before Margo responded. "I can meet you there in 15 minutes if that works for you."

He chuckled. "It does. You caught me after the dinner rush. So I'm available now, and it's not dark yet. So that's a bonus."

"Yes, that is a bonus, I'll be there in 15 minutes."

The call ended, and he pocketed his phone. He nodded as he mumbled, "Yes, finally."

He'd already checked with the bank. He already knew he could afford it. He already knew that he would bid over what they were asking if need be. He'd find a way.

He walked outside to the few straggling diners eating or chatting. He didn't have music tonight, so he could step away for a few minutes.

But he wanted to be there and walk around outside before Margo got there.

"Hey, Jace, how are you?" A couple of ladies called out.

"Hey, ladies, looking good. How was the meal?" The table of four, two couples that he'd often seen here, nodded in appreciation. The taller of the two men said, "Dinner is great as usual."

The girls smiled and flashed their eyelashes. He chuckled. He loved flirting with the women just so far as to make them want to come back for more.

He stopped at a couple of other tables, flirted a little bit, and moved on. He strode through the inside, stopped at the bar, and waited for his bartender, Mason, to be free. Customer service was first and foremost. Always.

Mason refilled the customer's drinks and turned to see him at the end of the bar. "Mason, I'm going to be out for just a few minutes. I'll be back shortly. You got this, right?"

"Got it, boss."

Jace walked out the front door feeling confident in his staff and this new venture. He sauntered next door to the thrift shop and walked around the entire outside. He didn't see anything scary.

The landscaping wasn't much, but he wasn't worried about that anyway. He was more worried about, well, what was he worried about? He was going to tear the building down, so none of it mattered.

He didn't want to make it too easy, though, either, because then they might hold out for more money. He wanted this place, but he also wanted a deal.

A pearl white SUV showed up, a Lincoln no less. Nice.

Margo Price stepped from the SUV looking confident and business-like with her white slacks, her yellow billowing top, and her purse. He recognized her from being at the Sandbar after her husband's funeral with her sisters. Now he understood why it took her a couple of days to get back to him.

He walked forward and reached out his hand to shake hers. "Nice to meet you, Margo. Formally meet you, anyway. I'm Jace Marriott."

"It's nice to formally meet you, too. I believe you waited on my sisters and me the other night."

"I sure did."

She nodded. "The food was good."

"Thank you for that."

"You're welcome."

He hurried to offer his condolences. "I would just like to say I'm sorry for your loss."

He saw her jaw tighten. "Thank you." She took a deep breath, "Shall we go in?"

She said it all too quickly. Who was he to judge? People handled their grief differently. He'd lost a lot of friends in the service, and he handled each one a little differently, and they weren't his spouse. So he wasn't about to judge anyone else's grief.

Margo stepped to the door, unlocked the realtor lock-box, took the key out, and unlocked the deadbolt on the thrift shop. She opened the door and reached in to flip on the lights. She pulled open the shades and said, "Well, as you can see, things are as is. The tables, everything that's here is just the way it is. The owner has already left town and simply wants a quick sale."

He looked around, trying to look interested, but who was he kidding? He didn't care two shits about what the building looked like.

"I'll take it," he said. "I'd like to write an offer right now."

She cocked her head to the side slightly, "All right then, a man who knows what he wants."

"That's right, I'm a man who knows what I want, and right now, I want this building."

She shook her head a couple of times and chuckled. "Well," she looked around, "there aren't any chairs or anything to sit on in here."

"How about if we go next door to the bar, I'll buy you a drink. Can we write out the offer and get it taken care of right away? I'm prepared to give you earnest money, which is over there anyway."

She hesitated a moment and stared at him. He was a little puzzled by her look. She was beautiful. When she looked at him now, she had the most beautiful blue eyes; he hadn't noticed them the other night. Her dark hair complimented those blue eyes perfectly. She was slender, tall, tallish anyway, five foot six or so he'd say. She wore a white beaded necklace to match her slacks, a yellow and white bracelet, and the handbag that she carried matched her clothing.

She was a very polished-looking woman.

Finally, she said, "All right, we can do that. I'll just step out to my car quickly to get my laptop, and then I'll meet you inside."

"That sounds great." He stepped out of the front door

and waited as she locked it. Then she walked on the sidewalk, her heels clicking. That's when he noticed that her heels matched her slacks perfectly. You could barely see them. He chuckled to himself. He was still wearing shorts and sandals from working today. Sometimes when he worked out on the beach a lot, he kicked his flip-flops off and just went barefoot.

He loved this business that he was in. Who wouldn't? He wore shorts and flip-flops or sandals every day. Beautiful women surrounded him with bikinis and short shorts. He was living everybody's vacation. People came in in good moods, except for Margo and her sisters last night.

The majority of people who frequented his place were jovial and happy and looking to have a good time. He was right there for all of it. Every time the cash register chimed, he had to stop himself from grinning.

He stepped into the bar, walked around the back, and got himself a glass of water. Then he picked a table in the corner and set the glass of water down. Checking the shades on the windows to make sure there was appropriate light for her to write or type or whatever she was going to do with this offer, and then waited for her.

It was hard to sit still. When he was here, he was usually running around, getting drinks, serving food, picking up dishes, and chatting with the customers. That's how his business grew so quickly. Customers loved talking to the owner. They loved seeing the owner hustle. And, he had hustle worked out. It kept him trim. Shit, he regularly walked twenty-five to thirty thousand steps every day. Usually while carrying something.

The door opened, and Margo walked in. If the jukebox had been playing right now, that would be the song he always associated with Margo. Her long, dark hair flowed over her shoulders. It had to be warm with all that hair cascading around her. But, damn, it sure looked amazing. The white heels and slacks hung on her trim frame delightfully. The yellow was such a contrast to her dark hair he had a hard time looking away. His mouth dried, and all he could do was wave her over. He took a deep breath as she sat, her back was ramrod straight. She looked almost uncomfortable.

"What can I get you to drink, Margo?"

"I'll just take a water."

"Are you sure? Whatever you want is on the house."

"I'm working, so," she said

"I have iced tea if you'd like that. We have raspberry and regular. I've got a variety of sodas. It doesn't have to be alcoholic."

She finally smiled and he felt sucker punched. She was gorgeous when she smiled. As in, *Oh my gosh*, absolutely gorgeous.

"All right, I'll take a raspberry iced tea, please, and thank you."

"Coming right up." He hustled behind the bar as she pulled her laptop out. Watching from the corner of his eye, he noticed she got right to business.

She didn't waste time looking around, and she didn't seem to be interested in dawdling either. Excitement and nervousness coursed through his body.

He'd been working here after all, and finally, the owner decided to sell. A quick handshake deal and then a rapid, "We'll meet you at the bank, get the money, and I'll take off."

Within a week, this bar was his. And he'd busted hump since that day.

He set Margo's raspberry iced tea on the table and sat down across from her. She typed on her laptop for a few minutes. At least it seemed that long, and he started to feel foolish sitting there waiting for her to finally address him. Then he was irritated with himself for sitting here like a lap dog begging for a treat.

She finally started asking him questions. "The asking price on this place is one hundred twenty-five thousand. I know the owner is motivated. I also know there's one other person who has inquired."

He shook his head, "What are you saying? Do I need to offer more than the one hundred twenty-five thousand? Has that other person put an offer in?"

"Well, I'm not allowed to tell you that. I do work for the seller. I'm just telling you one other person is also interested."

"Okay. How about this? Offer five thousand more. Quick sale, cash, I can get the money tomorrow. No contingencies. I don't need an inspection. I'm actually going to bulldoze the place down."

Her eyebrows shot up. "Really? What are you going to do with it?"

"I'm going to expand my bar. My food business has gone crazy. We need more room in the kitchen, and I'd like the bar here to be wider so we can accommodate more people. And I need a buffer per the town council of thirty feet around the perimeter, and I don't have that with that building standing there. So I need it."

"All right. That sounds impressive. It sounds like you've thought about this quite a bit."

"I certainly have. And if that person, the other interested party, makes an offer more than mine, will someone let me know so that I can counter?"

"Well, the owner will let you know whether or not they accept or reject the offer, and if there is a counteroffer, they will counter your offer with, I assume, more than what the other offer is for."

"Okay. So it's not just going to be sold out from under me without me getting the opportunity to make another offer."

"No. It won't be sold from under you without allowing you the opportunity to make another offer. Once you have an offer in play, we'll see it through. Though if the owner outright rejects your offer, there isn't anything in play."

"Perfect."

Margo typed out things she needed. "So you don't need an inspection. You don't need a financing contingency. You just want it as is?"

"Yes, that's correct. I'm fine with all of it. The only thing I want is a clear title."

Margo nodded. "It has a clear title. I've already confirmed that with the title company, so you should be set to go."

She handed him a little handheld computer that looked like a bulky phone, it was connected to her computer. "When the X appears on the screen, please go ahead and sign your name. This is the actual offer. Closing next week. Cash. No contingencies. No inspection."

The X appeared. He quickly signed his name with his finger.

"And then this is the inspection report. Not that you need it, but I have to prove that I showed it to you."

She slid the Inspection Report across the table to him. "When the X appears, please sign that screen."

He glanced at the Inspection Report and signed his name as the X appeared.

She had a couple more forms for him to sign. Something about sewer inspection or whatnot because they're close to the beach. He didn't care about any of that, so he signed his name on all of them. And then she said, "And finally, you're giving the owner until this time tomorrow to accept or reject your offer."

"Yes, ma'am. Twenty-four hours."

She smiled and took her hand-held device back after his final signature. Her fingers brushed his lightly, and that gave him a little thrill. It didn't seem to affect her in any way, shape, or form. Maybe he was losing his touch. Women normally liked it when he flirted a little bit.

That brushing of the fingers. That was always a little flirt mode, wasn't it? Then again, she'd just recently lost her husband, so she was grieving.

She packed up her laptop. Then she finished her iced tea. "Thank you for the iced tea. Are you sure I can't pay for it?"

"I'm sure. It's on me. Come back again. I'll buy you another one. Especially if you come to tell me that my offer has been accepted."

She laughed.

He stared.

She stood and swept her hair over her shoulder. Then she strode out the door.

And he watched every single step she took. Until the door closed behind her.

6

Margo climbed into her SUV and took a couple of deep breaths. Did Jace Marriott think just because he was handsome and flirty that she'd just fall at his feet?

She closed her eyes. Is that what Logan did? Is that how he met Sierra Stigler? What about her anyway? Margo hadn't slept much last night. She'd stayed awake way too late reading through Logan's texts with Sierra. Half the time she told herself not to read them anymore. It was just making her sadder and madder. Then the other half of the time, she wanted to know exactly what was going on in his mind. Since she couldn't ask him and kick him in the nuts, the only thing she could do now was to read what he was telling Sierra and what she was telling him. When she got to the part where Sierra said,

> I love you so much, Logan, I can't wait to see you tonight.

and when he replied

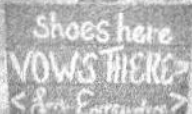

> I love you so much, Sierra, I wish we were together all the time.

She nearly threw his phone across the room.

Wish they were together all the time. Why hadn't he fucking divorced her? Why did he play this game? Then she picked up her phone and looked at that date on her calendar and saw that it was the weekend that Logan had said he was going fishing with his friends. He was fishing all right, but it wasn't with his friends, and it wasn't for fish. She bristled again and once more thought she should probably stop reading these texts. But part of her, the morbid part of her, needed to know exactly what was going on. How would she ever find out if she didn't read these insidious texts? And quite frankly, she felt like it was making her stronger. The more she hated Logan, the less she mourned him. Actually, right now, the only thing that she was mourning was the fact that she couldn't tell him off. That she couldn't make him look her in the eyes and tell her what he was doing. That's what made her the maddest right now. There was going to be no closure for her. How would she ever get that? She let out a deep breath and started her SUV. She pulled away from the Sandbar, turned around in the parking lot, and pointed her SUV in the other direction to head back toward her office.

When she entered the office her receptionist Addison smiled. It wasn't a complete smile. It didn't reach her eyes. It was a pitying smile. She was really getting tired of the pitying smiles, and she didn't even think Addison knew about Logan's affair. "Hi, Margo I have a couple of messages here for you."

She handed her two sheets of pink paper. Margo glanced at the names; they were from two of Logan's sellers.

"More, *I'm so sorry about your loss,* and *how are we gonna handle this?*" phone calls. She felt like she'd answered a hundred of them today, but truth be told, Logan didn't have that many deals in the pipeline. When she thought about it now, she'd been working her ass off. He was the one out playing all the time with Sierra.

"Thank you, Addison. I just wrote an offer on the thrift shop. I'm going to call Lorraine to see if she wants me to fax it or email it to her."

"Oh, that's fantastic! Congratulations."

"Thank you." She strode into her office and closed the door. She sat at her desk, and while she was thinking about it, she decided to pull up their software and see the ongoing real estate deals that she had versus the ongoing real estate deals that Logan had. She waited a few minutes for the information to populate, and just as she had expected, she had twenty-five deals in the works, either as a listing agent or offers. Logan had eight, so she hadn't taken a hundred phone calls today, it only felt like it. Eight. Logan had eight. Man, she was all kinds of stupid for supporting his sorry, cheating ass. No wonder he didn't leave her. He'd have actually had to work. Deciding not to get all morose and pissed off one more time, she called the owner of the thrift shop, who was a nice little lady named Lorraine. She'd moved out of state to live closer to her children, and Margo knew she'd be happy with Jace's offer. Deciding she should get this deal wrapped up right away to keep her mind in the right frame, she set her sights on that. The other buyer who had been somewhat interested was working with another agency. Margo, being the listing agent, and the selling agent, would get the entire commission. Part of her bristled that it would be too easy for Jace Marriott. Everything was probably easy for Jace Marriott. He was handsome. He was built. He had a great personality. He enjoyed his job. She watched him saunter through the restaurant and outside on the beach, stopping and talking with his customers and flirting with the ladies. You could tell he liked what he was doing, and then that brought her right back around to Logan. Did he like what he was doing? And then she wondered how he met Sierra. Was it because she had called about selling a business or selling a home? She looked her up in the computer system. Nope, she didn't see anything like that. She shouldn't dwell on it, but it was bugging her. The constant vacillation between getting past this and dwelling on it was giving her a headache.

She tapped Lorraine's number and waited as it rang. "Oh, hello Margo, how are you?"

"I'm fine, Lorraine. How are you doing? Did you get your unpacking finished?"

"Pretty close. I only have a couple of little boxes left. I didn't have much, you know. I didn't need to bring furniture or anything. My daughter has everything I need right here, so there wasn't much to unpack, but I'm settling in nicely. How can I help you?"

Margo sat back in her chair and tried to relax her shoulders. "I received an offer on your thrift shop. It's a good offer, to be honest with you. A hundred and thirty thousand, five thousand over asking."

"Oh goodness, that's fantastic and so fast. Thank you so much, Margo. Yes, I'm happy to accept that offer."

"I do believe there was one other interested party. Did you think we should wait and see what their offer would be like?" Margo closed her eyes. She shouldn't ask clients that. She should get this deal done and done now.

She was kind of losing her edge here. The old Margo would have had this deal closed already.

"Nope, if we have an offer, I'm happy to get it signed and get everything settled. And five thousand over asking, my goodness, that's fantastic. That old building needs a lot of work."

"My understanding is he's going to tear it down."

"Oh dear. Well, can't blame him for that, I guess. Like I said, it needs a lot of work."

"Right, so okay, how do you want to receive this offer? I can email it to you. I can fax it to you. You let me know what works best for you."

"Oh honey, why don't you just email it over? I think you have that e-sign thing. I can sign it that way, right?"

"Yes, I can send it over for an electronic signature. We can get it wrapped up right away, but you have twenty-four hours to accept if you want to think about it."

Lorraine laughed. "If I didn't know better, I would think you were trying to talk me out of this, Margo."

"No. No, no, I'm not trying to talk you out of it I just don't want you to feel pressured."

She closed her eyes again. She had to stop trying to ruin this deal. It was a done deal. It was an easy commission. She should be happy with that. "Okay, I'll email it over as soon as we hang up, and if you have any questions about the offer at all, just give me a call or respond to the email. I'll wait to get your signature back."

"Thank you, dear. I sure do appreciate it. After all you've been through recently, I certainly didn't expect things to move this quickly."

Margo took a deep breath. "Well, as they say, life goes on right? Logan died. I didn't, and I have a business to run so..."

"Oh, what a good positive attitude you have, Margo." If she only knew, she chuckled to herself. "When I lost my Jonny, I didn't know how I'd get out of bed in the morning, but we do. Mostly because we have to pee." She laughed. "Then, we have to eat. There are things to take care of, and before you know it, a week has passed. Then two. Then a month. We go on."

Margo closed her eyes. Exactly all of that. So far, that had been her life. Lorraine didn't know about the late nights reading love texts her husband had sent to another woman, but that would be her burden to bear.

"Alright, I'll get this over to you. Give me five. It was good talking to you, Lorraine."

"It was good talking to you, too, dear. I'll watch for your email. Goodbye."

Margo listened to the line go quiet and waited a moment. She set her phone on the desk and opened her laptop. She immediately emailed the offer over and tried not to bristle.

Jace Marriot seemed like the kind of man who would get what he wanted anyway, so it's not like she was in the mood for a big fight. She sent the email and let out a sigh. Maybe she should just go home for the day. Her sisters were still here, at least Carley and Holly were. Josseline left this morning.

Margo had apologized to her now that she knew why Josseline's attitude was so cross toward Logan. Josseline said she wouldn't go looking for an acting job. She was clearly unable to hide her emotions, and she so hated Logan for hurting her and lying to her.

She closed the lid on her laptop and packed it away in her bag. Picking up her purse and her computer bag, she strode out the door. "I'll see you in the morning, Addison. I'm going to go home and get some rest."

"You have a good night, Margo, I'll see you in the morning."

7

The next day, Jace was at his restaurant. The lunch crowd was filtering in, and the place was filling up. The weather was exceptionally hot outside, so most of his customers were inside. Once again, his mind ran to the offer on the building next door, which would help alleviate this predicament of people waiting in line. During the lunch hour, that was a killer. People had limited time to eat, and he needed to get them fed before they left for somewhere else.

Hopefully, his offer would be accepted today. For about the hundredth time he glanced at his watch, hoping Margo would call to tell him his offer was accepted. It was a fantastic offer, he knew that. She knew that. Hopefully, the owner would be overjoyed.

Delivering a plate to a group of ladies from the bank, who came in for their lunch hour every Friday, he grinned as he set their food in front of them.

"Ladies, looking good. We have the best-looking bank employees in the world."

They giggled. One of them crossed her arms over her ample chest and said, "I'll have you know I have a brain."

He laughed. "I have no doubt you are smart as a tack." She smiled, and Jace continued to the table next to theirs.

He took a food order and then turned to walk back to the kitchen, but he froze. Margo was standing in the doorway watching him.

Even the hair on the back of his neck rose at the look she was giving him. He nodded to her, took the order he had just taken to the kitchen, and then exited the kitchen to come back out to talk to her.

"Hello there. It's nice to see you."

"Oh, I'll bet it's nice to see me. You know it's offensive to women when you flirt like that."

Jace turned and looked at the happy faces in the crowd. Everybody was talking and laughing and eating their food.

"No one looks irritated. Which one? Point out which one is irritated with me."

"I didn't say there was anyone in particular. I just said it was offensive."

"You know, Margo, maybe if you'd lighten up, you'd have a little fun too. You seem to be a bit of a stick in the mud."

"I am not a stick in the mud."

"Really? Well, I can't imagine that you're much fun to be around. All you do is snap at me. And your shoulders are so stiff, and your jaw is so tight, it doesn't look like you've ever smiled."

"You're boorish."

"Well, maybe. But I'm fun."

Her eyes narrowed slightly, "Anyway, I delivered your offer to the seller, and she has accepted."

Margo pulled the offer from her bag. "Here's your copy. Closing's next week. Let me know the time of day you want to have the closing, and I'll have it arranged with the title company."

"Perfect. Thank you so much."

He looked the offer over quickly. "Did you want a raspberry iced tea or something a little stronger to help you loosen up a bit?"

"I don't need anything to loosen up a bit, Jace."

"Oh, I beg to differ. A beautiful woman like you should be smiling all the time."

"Maybe I have reason not to smile."

"Well, you might, but you're going to make a nice commission off of this sale, so that should be reason enough to smile. If it's not money, what is it?"

"Really, my personal life is none of your business. I'll be in touch about the closing." She turned and walked out, and Jace shook his head.

That woman was uptight.

As in Uptight.

Man. As he walked back to the kitchen, he saw Hanna and Quinn walking in.

"Hey there, you two. Are you here for lunch?"

Quinn grinned. "I sprung Hanna from the bakery. She doesn't get out for lunch much, but her mom was available today. So here we are."

"Fantastic. I'm sorry I don't have a table yet, but you can wait at the bar. It shouldn't be too long. Most people have to get back to work."

Hanna giggled. "I'm one of those people. Good thing my mom knows the bakery like I do. Maybe better."

He winked. "You get full service from the owner every day here, lady. As soon as I can get you a table."

She laughed and walked to the bar with Quinn, and he stepped back into the kitchen, took a drink of water out of the bottle he had sitting on the counter, and then went back out, rotating his neck.

His encounter with Margo had irritated him. He wasn't sure why. When he walked back out to the dining room, he stopped at the bar to make sure Quinn and Hanna had gotten drinks.

"What can I get you two?"

Quinn looked at him. "Everything okay?"

"Yeah. So good news, bad news, and good news."

"Okay." Quinn chuckled. "How about good news first?"

"All right. Well, I just made an offer on the thrift shop next door, and it was accepted today. So I'll need you to come and take a look at it for me so that we can make plans for expansion of the restaurant and the kitchen and tearing down the thrift store next door."

"Hey, buddy. Congratulations." Quinn reached out and shook his hand. "That's wonderful. What's the bad news?"

"Well, the bad news is, I don't know. I've offended Margo Price somehow, and she just came in to tell me about the offer being accepted, but apparently, she thinks I flirt too much or something."

Hanna nodded. "Well, I heard in the bakery that before Logan's death, they were on the rocks or something. She's probably kind of soured on men right now."

Jace nodded his head slowly. "Ah, that would make sense. She said I'm a flirt, and that's derogatory toward women, and that I -- well, basically that."

"I wouldn't take too much offense to it, Jace. I think she's going through a tough time right now. I was actually considering stopping in and talking with her, businessperson to businessperson, and I've known her for a few years, although it was back before I had returned home, so I thought maybe she could use a friend."

Jace nodded. "Well, that might help relieve her sour mood. After all, every time I see you, I smile."

Hanna smiled back, and Quinn grinned.

"All right, let's get your order taken, and then I'll feed you two. And Quinn, stop in and see me later on so we can talk about the expansion, either first thing in the morning or right after lunch, whatever your schedule will allow."

Quinn nodded. "Actually, Hanna and I were hoping we could come in this evening for dinner and talk to you about the wedding."

Jace nodded. "That'll work. Let's do it then."

8

———

Margo huffed off back to the office with the completed offer in her hand. Yeah, men were all alike, out for instant gratification. Throw away the old bag that you've been married to, who's devoted her life to helping you build this business. Yeah.

Just start new with the first tall, thin redhead that walks your way. She couldn't stand watching Jace flirt with the women in the restaurant. She couldn't stand the thought that he was just like Logan. Not that it mattered. She just needed to get this real estate deal done and move on. That's what she was going to do, dammit. She was going to make this real estate company the best real estate company in the state. That's what Logan had always said he wanted. She thought he was working toward that end, but he never accomplished it because he wasn't working toward it at all. She was going to work toward it now and show that lying, cheating piece of shit exactly how it was done.

She walked into the office and took a deep breath. "Hey Addison, I've got the offer signed, and we're all set and ready to go now. Please call the title company to get the closing paperwork set for next week. Let's target Friday, that will give them a week."

Addison smiled. "Sure thing, Margo. And you've got a couple of voicemails on your phone."

"Thanks, Addison."

Margo walked into her office, set her laptop on the desk, and opened it up. She picked up the receiver on her phone and listened to the first message.

"Hey, it's Carley. I'm just checking on you and wondering how things are going. If you need me to come back and stay with you for a while, I'm happy to do so just let me know. Love you. Call me when you get the chance. Bye."

She grinned. No, she'd be fine. She didn't want her sisters putting their lives on hold for her anymore. They'd been with her for nearly two weeks while Logan was in the hospital and after the funeral for a couple of days. She needed to do this on her own.

Logan had been dead all of four days now. Her sisters had gone home, and the house was empty. She knew she needed to start thinking about getting rid of his clothing. Maybe that's what she'd do tonight. She'd go home and toss all his crap out of the closet, so she didn't have to think about it, didn't have to look at it, and didn't have to do anything with it. That would be a good cleansing in more ways than one. That's what she would do. As that thought seeded itself in her mind, it grew. Soon, that's all she could think of doing. Better to get rid of any trace of him than to hang on.

Determined to make that her evening's project, she listened to the next voicemail.

"Hello, Margo, this is Jailisa Burns from Grant Park's office. Grant would like you to come into the office tomorrow at noon. He received a phone call from an attorney in Miami who has a copy of Logan's will and wants to discuss it. Please let me know if you can make it. Our number here is 555-1212. Thank you."

Logan's will? Did they still do a reading of the will? My god, she hadn't even thought of it. When did they have them done? Gosh, it was probably 20 years ago when they first started this business they'd gone in and had wills prepared. She probably had a copy of it somewhere at home. Why would she need to go in for a reading of the will? And how would an attorney in Miami have a copy? That didn't seem to make any sense at all.

She shrugged, picked up the phone, and called her sister Carley.

"Hey there, Margo, how are you?" Carley answered brightly.

"I'm good, just closed a real estate deal."

"Well, it didn't close, but I got the offers signed by the buyer and the seller, so we're all set. Closing's next week, how's that for a good week after a horrible week?"

Carley was quiet for a moment. "That's a good way, I guess, to end a terrible week. How about we say that?"

"Yep, that's a good way to say it. I'm with you on that. So, I'm thinking about going home and tossing all of Logan's stuff. I don't need you to come and help me. I don't want you to put your life on hold anymore, but that's what I'm going to do today, and I think it'll be therapeutic. I'm going to box it all up. Everything. And I'm going to take it down to the thrift store. Anybody who wants it can have it."

"Some of that equipment is worth some money, Margo. Maybe you want to reconsider that. Maybe you need to give yourself a little bit more time to process everything."

A sardonic laugh burst from her chest. "I don't need to process anything anymore. Basically, the last seven years of our lives were a lie. I'm not gonna hang on to anything from that bastard." She spun a pen on her desk as she talked. "Oh, and speaking of, I got a voicemail from my lawyer's office. I have to go in tomorrow at noon for a meeting with Grant and an attorney from Miami who claims to have a copy of Logan's will. So, I'm also going to be searching for our wills at home to bring in my copy. Isn't that weird?" Margo shrugged. But a hot pit was growing in her stomach the more time she had to think about it.

"Well, I suppose it's maybe a formality of his office. Maybe he just wants you to know how you have to proceed. After all, you guys have a business. It might be different for a business."

"I suppose that could be. Unless, on one of Logan's trips, he took his will down to Miami and consulted an attorney, how else would a Miami attorney have a copy of his will?"

Carley was quiet for a few moments. "Hang on," she quickly said. Margo could hear the tapping of computer keys in the background, and that pit in her stomach grew hotter. The silence dragged on, and Margo became uncomfortable. More than uncomfortable, she took a deep breath to alleviate the growing pain in her stomach.

"Carley?"

"Umm." Carley let out a long breath on the other end of the phone. "Margo, I just checked to see if you need to let your beneficiaries know of a change in a will in Florida. You don't."

That burning pit in her stomach erupted into a white-hot inferno. She stood abruptly as the inferno roared to life.

"That dirty son of a bitch. He had better not have handed over my share of anything to that slut he's been fucking."

"I'm coming to your place. I'll be there in a couple of hours."

Margo couldn't say anything. Her head spun, and she felt dizzy and nauseous. She planted her hand on the top of her desk as she tried to focus on anything in the room. Everything moved and spun. She ended up dropping her phone on the top of her desk and then bent over and retched into the wastebasket in front of her. She hadn't eaten much, so the only thing that came out was the bile in her stomach. She retched again as she dropped to her knees. Her head hung over the wastebasket, and she gripped it as if it were a lifeline.

After a few moments, she felt on the top of her desk for the tissue box. She blew her nose. Grabbing another tissue, she wiped around her mouth. Tossing that tissue after the other, she took in a slow, deep breath, grateful that the dizziness had subsided.

She heard Carley's panicked voice faintly and remembered her sister was on the phone. Getting herself to a standing position, she sat in her desk chair, and though her hand shook, she picked up her phone.

"I'm here, Carley," she managed to squeeze out.

"I'll be there in a couple of hours. Are you okay to drive home?"

"Yes."

"Get yourself home. I'll meet you there, and we'll figure out a game plan."

Margo was too depleted to say much more than "Okay."

Carley ended the call, and Margo leaned her head back and closed her eyes. She rested there for a few minutes. The ringing of the phone brought her around, and Addison's voice on the intercom interrupted her solitude.

"Margo, Jailisa from Grant Park's office is on the phone."

"Okay. Thank you."

She took a deep breath and steeled herself to take this call.

Picking up her desk phone she tapped the blinking line. "Hello, Jailisa, how can I help you?"

"Hello, Ms. Price."

"Margo. Call me Margo."

"I do apologize. Margo. I wanted to make sure you did receive my voicemail from earlier today. Grant wants to make sure you can meet here tomorrow at noon."

"Do you know anything more than an attorney from Miami is coming in?"

"I'm sorry. I don't. His office called ours this morning. They didn't even check to see that the time worked for Grant or yourself. It was more of a demand."

"That's concerning."

Margo closed her eyes and kept her breathing even.

"Maybe. It could just be their demeanor. Some attorneys are like little pit bulls. They think the world revolves around them. You and I are spoiled. We work with Grant, who is the nicest man I know. Besides my husband, that is."

Margo smiled, but her energy was zapped. "Yes. We're spoiled, alright." She sat forward. "I'll be there tomorrow at noon. Thank you for calling back again today. I did just get in a few moments ago and heard your voicemail but had return calls to make before yours."

Jailisa chuckled. "It doesn't matter to me, Margo. I just wanted to check once more before I leave for the day. I'll see you tomorrow at noon."

9

Jace stood outside the Sandbar looking at it from the road. He had a notebook in front of him and a pencil. He drew pictures in his notebook, scribbled a bit, scratched through his picture, and tried again. Quinn pulled up and waved. "I'll be right out." He called out and parked his truck in the lot alongside the Sandbar. Jace tried once more to capture the image in his head.

He wasn't an artist. He'd never been more than a modified stick figure kind of artist. But he couldn't sleep at night thinking about this remodel. That's what it was going to be - a remodel. At first, it was just an expansion, but he had a real opportunity right now to make it what he wanted. He wanted a new, fresh, happy atmosphere without the issues of old plumbing needing repair and old wiring giving him fits. He was going to make this place spectacular.

He glanced over to where Quinn had parked and now helped Hanna out of his truck. He kissed Hanna and she smiled at him. They were happy. Quinn had changed a bit since meeting Hanna. He seemed more relaxed. He smiled all the time now. And that was wonderful to witness. Sid had changed since meeting Grace, too. A little niggle of jealousy flared to life, but he took a deep breath and blew it out. Quinn and Hanna stopped next to him on the edge of the road. Quinn glanced over at his notebook.

"Drawing pictures now, are we?"

"Yes," Jace said. "Fuck you." He leaned around Quinn and looked at Hanna. "Not you. Your sarcastic husband."

Quinn chuckled. His arm wrapped around Hanna's shoulders, and he squeezed lightly.

"So, what are you trying to do here?"

Jace handed Quinn his notebook. "You try to draw it. I can't."

Quinn chuckled. "I'm not an architect, you know."

"I do know. But I also know you can draw buildings, and I can't speak to an architect without being able to adequately convey what it is I want."

Quinn nodded. "Okay. Let's see what we can do."

"Good. Okay. I want it to look like a Jimmy Buffet-style building. A place that people will stop at just because it looks like a place they want to be. We're on the water in Florida, so we should certainly have bright colors, palm trees, and surfboards hanging around. Tropical, fun, happy."

"Okay." Quinn absently said as the pencil he held crawled across the pages of the notebook. Hanna glanced at Quinn's drawing and smiled.

Jace continued to dream. "I'd like a covered patio to go around the two sides and the back looking out on the water. Ceiling fans that look like palm fronds should offer a gentle breeze. The tables on the beach should be made out of composite wood so they'll be durable but also heavy, so the winds don't send them flying. We have that issue with the tables we currently have. Teals. Oranges. Blue. White. Green. Colorful."

"Okay. I can't draw the colors, so that will come later."

Jace nodded. His excitement grew as Quinn massaged his imagination. "I want a Tiki Bar placed between the building and the water's edge. We'll sell drinks and light snacks from the Tiki Bar to people partying on the Sandbar, so they don't have to come all the way back to the bar. Also, outdoor guests can order out there."

"Sounds perfect." Hanna mused.

Jace grinned. "Also, I want lounge chairs in small groupings on the beach. Anyone coming to listen to music and wanting to relax will have the option of sitting at a table or lounging on the beach."

Quinn's lips turned up into a smile as he continued to draw. When he finally turned his notebook around, Jace's heartbeat increased. Quinn had done a great job of capturing the vision he had for the Sandbar. Close to it, anyway. It was a pencil drawing in black and white, but the basics were there.

"That's it!" Jace continued to stare at the drawing. He saw little squares under the tables. "What are those?"

"I thought we could build a floating deck off the building. The tables and chairs can sit on the floating deck, which will make it easier for customers to sit and waitstaff to serve."

"That's perfect."

"We can add posts here and there and string lights from them, but we can also add umbrellas to the posts that can be opened when the sun is high to shade guests."

Jace's right hand pressed against his chest. "You..." He didn't know what to say. "Perfect." That was all that would come out. "It's perfect."

Jace stared at the drawing Quinn had made. He reached over and took the notebook from his friend's hands. His heartbeat began to return to normal, but his heart swelled. "Thank you." He stared a bit more. "You've added a second story."

Quinn laughed. "You're welcome. Imagine the views."

"Right." He hadn't thought of a second story. But if he was going to go for it, he should go for it all the way. Go big or go home, as they said.

Hanna giggled. "Your face is one of bewilderment."

Jace grinned. "I think I'm feeling bewildered at the moment."

Quinn laughed. "Can you think right now? We'd like to come in and plan our wedding."

Jace tucked the notebook under his arm. He nodded toward the bar, "Yep. Let's go make some wedding plans. We'll get you married before we start digging into this building."

Entering the bar, he strode to his little office and tucked his notebook away into his computer bag. He'd take it home tonight for safekeeping. He grabbed his work notebook, the one he kept for customers and their parties, and strode back to the bar to find Quinn and Hanna chatting away with Mason.

Mason had been with him for a few weeks now and was doing well. A former Navy SEAL, he suffered terribly from PTSD. Staying busy seemed to be the key to keeping his mind from falling into despair. And Jace quickly began to rely on Mason to keep things even in the bar. He was a large man, over six-foot-five. Two inches taller than Jace himself. And while he smiled more now than he used to, he could also look imposing. Jace wished Mason had been around when those bikers came into town earlier in the year and wreaked havoc.

He lay his notebook on the bar and waited for his

friends to finish their chat with Mason. It gave him the advantage of seeing Mason in action when Jace wasn't running around doing everything else. Quinn asked Mason, "Where are you living?"

Mason frowned slightly. "I have an apartment out of town."

Quinn nodded and pulled out a business card. "Give me a call in about three weeks. We'll be close to renting or selling our first units in the old barracks in town. I'm converting them into housing. Only selling or renting to veterans."

Mason looked at Quinn's card and smiled. "Thank you. I've been hearing about this place. I'll give you a call."

Mason turned to see Jace watching. "Sorry, boss."

Jace shook his head. "Don't be sorry. Quinn is one of my best friends, and his beautiful future wife Hanna is good people. She's the cinnamon roll queen."

Mason laughed and patted his belly. "You're the person to blame for my extra couple of pounds."

Hanna laughed. "Guilty."

Mason nodded. "You're a tremendous baker."

Hanna's cheeks turned pink as Mason moved to help a customer on the other end of the bar.

"Okay folks, let's talk wedding plans."

Hanna smiled. "First, have you and Margo had any further conversation today?"

"No." It came out harder than it needed to be. "I've been in a good mood thinking about the remodel."

Hanna's lips turned down slightly. "Sorry to bring up the subject, but she really is very nice."

Jace shrugged his shoulders. "If you say so. She's more of a pain in the ass and judgy as far as I'm concerned."

Hanna frowned. Jace kept on. "She busts my balls at

every turn. She thinks I flirt too much. I'm untrustworthy. I told her she should lighten up, and maybe if she smiled once in a while, she'd have a little fun, too."

Hanna gasped and put her hand over her mouth. "Oh, my gosh, Jace. She's going through a tough time."

"That doesn't mean she should be rude."

"I doubt she means to be rude."

"Maybe I flirt a little bit, but that's just because I enjoy what I'm doing. And what's wrong with making women feel good about themselves? I don't see anything wrong with that."

"I plan on visiting her tomorrow with some cinnamon rolls. Just to check on her."

Quinn chuckled. "Your cinnamon rolls should make her smile."

Jace changed the subject. "Let's talk about your wedding."

Hanna grinned.

The door opened and Jace saw Sid and Grace enter the bar, hand in hand.

"Hey there, you two. I don't know if you guys knew this, but Quinn and Hanna came in tonight to talk about the wedding."

Grace hugged Hanna warmly, and Sid shook Quinn's hand. "That will be a great day for sure."

Jace tamped down the bit of jealousy these four shared and asked, "Are you partaking in the wedding conversation, or would you rather have your own table?"

Hanna turned to Grace. "Please join us. I'd love input. Since you've just gotten married, you have a lot to offer. If it isn't too boring for you."

"No, not boring at all."

Grace turned her face up to Sid. He grinned. "I'm in for that."

Jace led them to a table in the corner and made sure they had drinks. He happily sat at the table with his friends, notebook in front of him, and began jotting down the things Hanna and Quinn told him they wanted.

Hanna started. "We'd like a simple meal, buffet style, on the beach. We'd love the evening sun behind us. It'll be fantastic for pictures.

Jace asked, "What about decorations?"

"Gosh, I hadn't thought about decorations."

Grace chuckled. "How about if you let me help with that? I'd like to be involved in some way if I can."

Hanna nodded and smiled at her new friend. "You've got it. If you want to help with that, I'll be happy to take that help."

"Good," Grace laughed. "I'm happy to do that."

Sid leaned forward. "She's pretty good at decorating, so she won't let you down."

Hanna shook her head. "I didn't think for one second that she would let us down, or I wouldn't have so eagerly accepted her invitation to help."

"Fair enough."

Jace found himself growing edgy. He had so much excitement running through him right now that he couldn't wait to get things rolling. It would be a long week.

10

The front door opened, and Carley called out, "Margo, I'm here."

Margo stopped tossing Logan's clothing in boxes and stepped from the bedroom to greet her sister. She hurried down the hallway, and Carley appeared around the corner and rushed into her arms. The instant her sister hugged her, Margo burst into tears. Carley's arms tightened around her, and that made her cry all the more. They held each other for a while, heart to heart, until Margo's tears finally subsided.

When she pulled away, she swiped at her cheeks with her fingers and looked around for a tissue. Pulling one from the box, she dabbed at her face. Carley did the same.

Carley took her hand and led her to the sofa. They sat side-by-side cleaning up their tears. Carley finally said, "That's the first time you've cried, Margo."

"No, it isn't."

Carley's smile was small. Almost a frown actually. "When did you cry? When Logan took his last breath, you stood there numb. The only time tears came to your eyes was when we were all here in the kitchen laughing, and you said the laughter made you cry because it had been so long since this place sounded happy."

Margo's head tilted to the side as she rethought all of the moments since Logan entered the hospital. "I hadn't realized."

"That comment stuck with me since then." Carley shifted and turned toward her so that they were facing each other. "Margo, aside from what you know about Logan's indiscretions, had you been happy before he died? You said this place hadn't seemed happy in a long time. Why?"

Margo swallowed. It felt like her body deflated and her shoulders sank. "I don't know why I said that."

Carley took her hands and held them in hers. "Tell me the last time you and Logan laughed. Really laughed."

Margo swallowed the large knot that formed in her throat. She took a deep breath, but nothing came to her. Her eyes watered again, and she blinked furiously to stem the flow. Staring into her sister's pretty blue eyes, she swallowed again. "I can't recall." She sniffed. "That's even sadder than Logan passing. It has been a very long time since he and I sat here and had a good conversation."

"I wondered. You used to enjoy an evening drink out on the deck. When was the last time the two of you did that?"

Margo took a deep breath. So deep her lungs burned. She let it out slowly. She nodded her head slowly. "It's all making sense now, isn't it?"

"Well, you didn't go out and have an affair, that's not excusable. But it does seem that you two grew apart and were living separate lives."

"All my life consisted of was working."

Carley frowned. "Well, now you can make a change in that regard."

Margo snorted. "I guess."

Carley squeezed her hands. "What were you doing back there?"

"Tossing his shit in boxes."

"Want help?"

"Sure. Want a glass of wine to go with it?"

"I'll never turn down a good glass of wine."

Margo stood and pulled Carley's hand so her sister stood, too. They moved together, hand-in-hand to the kitchen. Margo pulled a bottle of wine from the wine fridge, while Carley pulled two wine glasses off the hanging rack above the far counter. She opened the bottle. They both giggled when the cork offered a little 'pop'. She poured them each a generous glass of wine and Carley held hers out. "I propose a toast to a new life. One filled with love and laughter and fun."

They clinked their glasses together and took a drink. Margo nodded. "Okay, let's get that bastard's clothes out of my house."

They strode to the bedroom where a stack of unopened boxes lay on the bed and several opened and taped boxes stood on the floor.

"Are you organizing the clothes in any certain way?"

Margo grabbed a handful of clothes from the closet, hangars and all. "Yes." She turned and dropped the clothes into a box, shoved the parts that didn't drop into the box inside, and stood proudly to look at her sister's smiling face. "Just like that."

Carley clapped her hands. "Yes! I love it."

They both grabbed armloads of clothes and shoved them into boxes. As they needed a new box, one of them would open a new one and tape the bottom.

As soon as Logan's clothing was packed, Margo grabbed her glass of wine and a box. "On to his bathroom shit."

Carley followed her, laughing, but she carried what was left of the bottle of wine. It didn't take them long to clean out Logan's shaving cream, aftershave, and some of his medicines. He had bottles and bottles of antacids. Margo tossed in three bottles of them and clapped her hands together. "Looks like his stomach was bothering him. Hope it hurt."

Carley stopped what she was doing and stared at her. Margo shrugged. "He was probably having stress-induced acid reflux. Guess lying is more hazardous to your health than we thought."

Carley stared a bit longer, then a smile crawled across her face. She burst out laughing and Margo joined her. And it felt good.

They finished off that bottle, then opened another one. Carley called the local thrift store to see if they could send someone over in the morning to pick up all these boxes. They said they'd have someone there at eight.

Their last stop was the basement, where they started tossing Logan's lures and bobbers into boxes. Then Margo said, "I'm sick of doing this. I'm calling a couple of his customers that he worked with a lot..." She pulled Logan's phone from her back pocket and tapped it a couple of times. "Yes, here he is. Nathan."

She tapped his name, and the phone began to ring. "Hello?" His voice sounded suspicious, and Margo chuckled. "Hi, Nathan, it's Margo. I suppose I gave you a start when I called you on Logan's phone. I'm sorry for that."

"Oh, well, yes a start is a good way to put it. How can I help you?"

"I'm getting rid of all of his lure and bobber-making stuff. Would you like it?"

"What? You mean you're selling it?"

"Nope. You can have it. But you have to take all of it."

"Oh...well...I'm...wow. I'd love it. But it must be worth so much..."

"It isn't worth anything to me. I'd like to get it out of the house actually. If you want it, I'd ask that you come by tomorrow and pick it up. I have boxes here."

"Oh. Um. I don't know what to say. Yes, I'll bring my son to help me. Does ten work for you?"

"Ten will be perfect. I'll see you then."

She hung up the phone and took another sip of wine. Carley smiled. "What else can we get rid of?"

Margo burst out laughing and replied. "How about another bottle of wine?"

Jace stopped at the Town Hall office inside the courthouse. The clerk behind the counter smiled. "How can I help you?"

"I need to file the paperwork to have the town council consider the expansion of my business at next week's meeting please."

"Oh, of course." She stepped away and pulled some papers from an organizer on the far wall. She strode to the counter and lay the papers in front of him. She pointed to the top sheet. "This is the application. You need to fill this out." She reached over and pulled a pen from a cup on the counter. "This next sheet is the detail behind your request. Fill it in as fully as you can."

"Okay."

The clerk pulled the last sheet from the pile. "This is the time of the meeting and location and what's on the agenda so far. This sheet will be updated before next week's meeting on Monday night."

"Okay. Thank you."

He moved to the small table at the back of the room and

sat in the metal folding chair pushed up to it. He filled out the application using the neatest handwriting he had. More than once, he wondered if he should have asked for this to be emailed to him so he could have filled it out on his computer. But he was here now.

After the mind-numbing process of filling out an application and asking detailed questions in minutiae, he finally walked back to the bar. He'd opted for walking today, not that he wouldn't get thousands of steps in later, but as a way to reconnect with the town. Often, he lived in his own little world at the bar.

He felt pretty good about this application, and as he walked back to the bar, he noticed that the buildings around the square had second stories. There's no reason his couldn't. And as he stopped and looked at it now, staring at his building from the road, the building did block the view of the beach, but that wouldn't change. And a second story wouldn't change that either. He turned with his back to the sandbar and looked at the roadway behind him. There weren't any buildings back there whose view would be blocked. There were palm trees that hid his home, but there was nothing else. The Sandbar stood on Sunset Beach Road, and Main Street was a block over. His house was in between, sort of, and the only other building next to the thrift shop was the fire department, and that was absolutely a two-story. Plus, when it came to noise, the fire trucks leaving were plenty noisy, much noisier than his music. As he looked down Sunset Beach Road to the right, he had his little bungalows along the right of the road, and Grace's little bungalows were further down on the left. Jamie Hart's place and the barn and, finally, Sid and Grace's house way up on the bluff. He wouldn't be blocking any of those places' view. And his friend Quinn, well he lived across the road from Sid and Grace's at the bottom of the bluff. He didn't have a view this way, so it wasn't going to block anything, was it?

He felt pretty confident about his request, and then excitement surged through him. Oh, he couldn't wait to get this going. Somewhere deep, deep down, this had been inside all along.

Things were finally coming to fruition. He couldn't be more excited.

He strode into the bar and began to prep for the lunch crowd. He was tending bar until Mason came in at five today. Normally, he waited tables and served lunches, but Mason had something going today. It was going to be a hot one, so being inside at the bar wasn't all bad. As he began pulling clean glasses from the dishwasher rack, the bar door opened, and he had to stop and stare for a moment. A tall, lanky redhead with long wavy red hair flowing down her back sauntered in with another man. The man wore a dark suit which seemed at odds with the weather. His build could be described as portly. His hair was balding, and they couldn't have been more of an opposite duo if he had imagined them himself. The redhead wore a tight black sleeveless dress and a diamond necklace. She was curvy and stunning. She noticed him staring, and her smile grew wide. She winked at him, and he grinned. She sauntered to a table with her companion, and they sat. He waited a beat, then went over to the table to take their order.

"What can I get you, folks?"

The redhead smiled at him, her right shoulder rose, and her head tilted. She was flirting with him. In front of her companion.

Her red lips turned up in a smile and before she spoke, she slowly swiped her tongue along the inside edge of her lips. "I'd just like an iced tea please."

He swallowed. "You got it."

He turned to her companion who seemed uninterested in anything, including the redhead, which he thought was funny. "I'll just take a coffee if you have it."

"Yes, sir we have coffee. Coming right up."

As he walked away, his confusion grew but who was he to judge? He prepared her iced tea, poured the gentleman a coffee, and brought creamers and sugar to the table with it. "Will you be having lunch with us?"

The man nodded. "Yes. What do you have for a special today?"

Jace nodded. "Let me get you some menus."

He strode to the podium near the front door, where the hostess would be standing as people came in for lunch, and pulled two menus from the rack. He laid one in front of each of his guests and said, "Our special today is fish and fries. It's a recipe from my own family, and folks around here seem to think it's pretty good. If you're not into seafood, we also have a mushroom Swiss burger on special today. Both are $2 off and come with fries, or you can substitute onion rings. We also have chicken noodle and beef barley soup. I'll give you a few moments to look over your menus."

He sauntered back to the bar and continued unloading the clean glasses from the dishwasher rack. His mind floated back and forth between the expansion, and how he would broach the town hall committee. They could be sticklers sometimes, and he wanted to formulate his argument if they gave him any grief. Now that Quinn had drawn the second story, he couldn't see his bar any other way. Quinn was right, the view would be phenomenal.

The redhead and her companion closed their menus, so he sauntered over to them. "What can I get for you, folks?"

They both ordered the mushroom Swiss burgers. She

continued to flirt with him by tilting her head, lifting her shoulders, and smiling while staring into his eyes. He thought it was weird that her companion didn't seem to notice, or care, shaking his head as he moved toward the kitchen.

He tucked their order on the cook's rack and called out, "Order up!"

Stepping out to the bar he continued to formulate his argument for the town council meeting.

12

A knock sounded on the front door. Margo stared at herself in the full-length mirror in her bedroom. White slacks and a flowing white sleeveless top with tiny blue flowers on it were what she'd chosen this morning. More due to the heat than anything. She turned to answer the door, but her sister Carley rushed out of the spare bedroom.

"I'll get it."

Margo halted and decided to dig through the safe at the back of her closet. That's where they kept all of their important documents. The business incorporation papers, estate planning, deed to the house and business. All of it was in there for fire and theft protection.

She dug to the back of the safe and found the deep blue folder where her estate planning documents were safely tucked inside. She opened it to confirm the contents. Margo Elizabeth Price was typed in bold letters. She knelt to reach further to the back. The other deep blue folder containing Logan's estate documents was not in there. A pit grew in her stomach. She had a feeling this was not going to be a good day for her again. Another crap to be taken on the top of Margo, just as the past two weeks had done to her. She stepped from the bedroom, hugging the blue folder to her body, and heard Carley speaking to another woman.

As she entered the living room she saw Hanna Valentine. She hadn't seen Hanna in years.

"Hi Hanna, how are you?"

"I'm good, Margo. I came to, well, bring you these."

Hanna held out a little pink box in front of her. "I made these cinnamon rolls. I'm not sure if you're aware, but I'm back in town and running my grandmother's bakery. Mom retired. But I revived grandma's cinnamon roll recipe and they've been a hit in town, so I thought I'd bring you some as an offer of condolences and friendship."

Margo's heartbeat increased. Here was sweet Hanna Valentine offering her gifts of condolences, and all Margo wanted to do was kick Logan in the balls. "Well, thank you, Hanna. That's very nice of you."

"I know this can be a hard time. But I wanted to offer you a shoulder, if you needed one, although it looks like..." Hanna turned to Carley. "You have a great one right here. But if you ever need someone to speak with, I just wanted to let you know I'm here. My friend Grace also." Hanna smiled, then rushed to continue. "Which by the way, I'm not sure if you're interested, but tonight my fiancée, Quinn Kurtz, from Kurtz Construction Company..."

Margo smiled, "Yes, I know Quinn. I just helped him with the barracks deal."

"Yes, that's right." Poor Hanna seemed frazzled or nervous. "Well Quinn and his friend Sid, who owns Miracle Garage on Main Street, will be at the Legion with area veterans, and Sid's wife Grace and I are going to the Sandbar to enjoy a couple of drinks. There's a band playing. Anyway, I'd like to extend the offer to you and Carley. Please join us. It's nothing formal. Casual dress. It's going to be a beautiful evening. The temperature is supposed to cool down to the mid-70s which will be perfect for sitting out on the beach and listening to some music."

Carley rushed. "Oh my God, that sounds like so much fun. Margo we've got to go. We need to get out of the house. Please let's go out."

Margo hesitated. She wasn't sure she'd be good company after whatever was about to happen at Grant Park's office.

Did it look right? So soon after Logan's death, did it look right for her to be out?

"I don't know if it would be right, so soon after Logan's death, doesn't it look like I'm out scouting the town?"

Carley shook her head. "You're single. Logan's been dead almost a week. The old rules don't apply these days and you are still alive. And having a drink with lady friends and listening to music isn't scouting. At least not the last time I checked."

She hesitated and bit her bottom lip. She wasn't ready to let the town know what Logan had been up to. It was embarrassing.

Hanna shrugged, "Well, I mean, I don't want to put pressure on you, but I wanted you to know that Grace and I will be there, and we will hold the table open for you too. If you care to join us. I hope to see you there."

She turned to leave, and Carley nudged Margo. "Let's go, Margo. Let's go."

Margo swallowed. "We'll see you there tonight, Hanna. Thank you for the invitation."

Hanna smiled brightly, "That's great. We're happy to have you join us. Seven o'clock."

"We'll be there."

"Jace. He's a friend of Quinn and Sid's. He saves us a table up near the stage. It's not right in front so the music isn't too loud. It's off to the side but we have a great view. Plus, we're close to the water. It's perfect."

At the mention of Jace's name, Margo flinched.

Carley seemed incredibly excited and rushed in. "Oh my gosh, that is so fun. Thank you so much for the invitation. We'll be there for sure. Right, Margo?"

She grabbed Margo's arm and squeezed tightly. Margo nodded woodenly. Maybe it would be fun.

"Yes, we'll be there at seven. Thank you for the invitation."

Hanna smiled and stepped out of the door and Margo turned to Carley. "I don't know if this is a good idea, Carley."

Carley shook her head. "Stop worrying about what anyone thinks. The old pearl clutchers aren't going to be there drinking and listening to music. And so what if they are? All that matters is that we know the truth. Right?"

Carley stepped in front of her. "We know the ugly truth."

"Yes, we do, and it is ugly."

"I agree with you. But you can't stop living. And actually, now more than ever you need to get out there and live again. You haven't been living in years, Margo. Not in years."

Tears threatened and Margo blinked furiously. She still gripped the folder in front of her. Taking a deep breath, she let it out. "I guess we better get going. And by the way, this is a copy of my estate planning documents. Logan's are missing from the safe."

Carley's shoulders dropped. "Oh dear. I dread this for you."

Margo shook her head and closed her eyes for a moment. When she opened them, she stared into her sister's eyes, similar to her own. "Don't dread it for me. I will deal with whatever he's done. But that fucker better not be trying to take my business away from me. I don't know how I'll get even, but I will."

Carley nodded. "Well, I like that attitude. Better to fight than it is to dwell in despair."

"I'm not desperate for anything. So this is just one more nail in the coffin, so to speak, for me to get past all of this. It seems as though Logan was hell-bent on ruining my life for whatever reason. I do not know. But I guess we better go find out."

"Okay."

Margo took a deep breath before she stepped inside Grant Park's office. She was still clutching the folder with her estate planning documents inside like it was a lifeline. She didn't even know why she brought it. Her documents weren't in question. Thankfully, Carley was with her.

Jailisa, Grant's personal assistant and receptionist, sat behind the front desk. She's always there. She's been there for years. For as long as Margo could remember anyway. "Good morning, Ms. Price or should I say afternoon. Good afternoon, Ms. Price."

Margo tried to smile but nerves forbid it. "Good after-noon, Jailisa. This is my sister Carley. Carley, Jailisa."

"Nice to meet you, Carley. I'll let Mr. Park know that you're here. Please take a seat."

Jailisa stood and then halted. "You know, on second thought, how about if you come right into the conference room? They followed her to the door to the right of her desk.

"Sit wherever you like. Can I get you water or coffee or anything?"

Margo shook her head. "No thank you. I'm good."

Carley nodded. "I'm fine also. Thank you though for the offer."

Jailisa stepped out and closed the door. Within seconds she heard Jailisa's voice outside. "Hello, how may I help you?"

Margo assumed the attorney from Miami stepped through the door and this was Jailisa's nice way of keeping them separate until they had to meet face to face. Margo swallowed, and Carly reached over, took her hand, and squeezed. "It's gonna be okay, Margo. We are going to deal with whatever, and I am here with you the entire way."

She looked into her sister's eyes. "Thank you, Carley. I honestly don't know what I would have done these past days without you. Actually the past couple of weeks. This is all so surreal. Certainly not something I ever dreamed I'd be dealing with."

"I don't think anybody dreams of dealing with anything like this, but just know you are not alone."

"I do appreciate it. Thank you."

The back door to the conference room opened and Grant Park stepped in. He wore a nice light gray suit with a blue tie. It looked friendly. "Good morning."

He reached over and shook Margo's hand, then he shook her sister's hand.

"This is my sister, Carley. Carley, Grant Park my attorney."

"It's nice to meet you, Carley."

Grant sat at the head of the table to Margo's right. Carley to her left.

"So the attorney from Miami is here. His name is Mathias Zsidai. I don't know what he wants to talk about, Margo, but what I want to caution you about is this. Whatever he says, try not to react too strongly. After he leaves, we will have a discussion, and we will talk about whatever it is that he has. He wouldn't share it with me over the phone, which I find in poor taste. Since he knows that you are my client, I can't imagine that he has anything that should be secret, but some attorneys like to keep people off-guard. That's probably what he's trying to do."

She swallowed the warm bile that climbed up the back of her throat and took a deep breath. "Okay, I kind of suspected overnight that this was bad news, and I did look this morning. She pushed the folder toward Grant. He'd recognize it of course, because he's the one who created their wills and powers of attorney years ago. "I found my estate documents but not Logan's. In our safe."

Grant didn't say anything. He pressed his lips together and nodded. "Okay. Well, you tell me when you're ready."

"Let's get it over with," Margo said.

Grant stepped out of the room. He was gone for a few minutes, but it felt like hours.

Soon, he stepped in with a portly man with dark thinning hair. He wore a dark suit and a green tie. He had round, dark-rimmed glasses, and she wondered why on earth a professional man would wear glasses that looked like that. It was almost comical with the roundness of his body and head.

He shook her hand. "My name is Attorney Mathias Zsidai."

"I'm Margo Price. This is my sister, Carley."

He shook both of their hands and then sat down. He pulled a folder out of his briefcase. It looked similar to the one Margo had brought in, but this one was black, not blue.

"Mr. Price," he stopped and looked at her, then looked back down at the folder, "came in to see me two years ago.

He had some changes made to his will and I understand he has now passed."

Margo nodded slowly. "Yes, he passed five days ago."

"Well, I'm not sure if he was lucid before he died or if he shared anything with you of a...a sensitive nature or if I am the bearer of this news."

Margo squared her shoulders. "If you mean, did he tell me that he had been having an affair for the last seven years? No, he didn't tell me."

Grant Park looked at her. His eyes rounded. He said nothing. His expression was of a man who was stunned. Margo continued.

"My sister found out by looking at his phone while he lay dying. His phone continued to chime. The texts were coming in. She checked the texts and found that they were from Sierra Stigler. Upon looking further into Logan's phone, I see that Logan and Sierra Stigler have been seeing each other for seven years."

Mathias blustered, "Yes, yes, that's my understanding as well. And when Mr. Price came in, he wanted to have an amendment made to his will. Upon his death, well here let me see..." he opened the folder and pulled a will from inside. Since he sat directly across from Margo, she saw Logan's name, upside down, in bold on the document. *Logan Price, Last Will and Testament.* He cleared his throat and continued lifting the cover page of the will. "Two years ago, Mr. Price came into my office with Ms. Stigler, and he asked to have an amendment made to the will. Upon his death, Mr. Price has given ten percent of Price Realty to Ms. Stigler."

Margo's stomach turned, but ten percent was better than fifty percent, so she would take that. She tried not to show the relief she felt. She simply folded her hands together on top of the table and waited for him to continue.

Attorney Zsidai continued. "Accordingly, Mr. Price also wanted me to convey to you that he would like Ms. Stigler to have a place in Price Realty as his last request. They were very much in love, and he wanted to include her in his business."

Margo knew that Logan seemed to have loving feelings towards Sierra, and she conveyed the same in their texts. She'd read them, ad nauseam, the last few nights. But she didn't say anything. At the moment, the anger that brewed in her gut wouldn't offer anything good coming out of her mouth. Grant Park finally found his voice, and took the document from Attorney Zsidai, and looked it over. "May I have this? Is this a copy, or do you need me to make a copy?"

Attorney Zsidai responded, "That's your copy, I have the original here."

Grant nodded. "Thank you. My client and I will converse if you'd like to step back into the other conference room while we talk. You're welcome to do that. If you prefer to leave and have me, call you, that's certainly up to you as well."

Attorney Zsidai stood. "I'll go talk to my client."

Margo's head spun. Sierra Stigler was here? Sierra Stigler wanted to be part of Price Realty? That was not going to happen. Attorney Zsidai left the room and closed the door.

Grant closed Logan's will. He folded his hands over the top of it and said, "How long have you known about this Margo?"

" Carley and my other two sisters found out while Logan was dying. They didn't tell me until the day of the funeral. I've been reading those texts each night before I go to bed. It solidifies in my gut that Logan has indeed been having an affair with Sierra Stigler, and it has indeed been going on for about seven years. Every time a shoe drops or a bomb drops, it's a nail in Logan's coffin, as far as I'm concerned. I admit I was immediately shocked, and then again, it's weird because I wasn't. As I started reading the texts and comparing the dates with my calendar, when Logan lied that he was going fishing, or playing golf, or he was looking up this business, or he was writing an offer on that business, he was with Ms. Stigler. As I realized how much that lying son-of-a-bitch has actually lied to me, it's giving me more peace."

Grant nodded slowly, "I understand. Well, I'd like to point out a couple of things here if you haven't already figured it out. Logan was a fifty percent owner in Price Realty. He cannot give ten percent of your fifty percent, he can only give ten percent of his fifty percent, which means that all she will own is ten percent of fifty percent or overall, only five percent. The percentage is nil, to be honest with you, and she has no right to ask to be part of the real estate company. She has no voting rights. She does not have any right to anything other than a five percent share of the overall company, which you would only have to offer an accounting and a check once a year after taxes are done."

Margo swallowed.

"Okay so I need to ask you, Margo, how do you want this to play out as to Sierra Stigler being part of the company and working there?"

"No, she will not be part of my company. It's my company. As a matter of fact, for the last seven years, while Logan was off fucking her, I was working my ass off to build that company. Price Realty is, in actuality, Margo Price, not Logan Price, not Margo and Logan Price, it's Margo Price. I did a little looking when I got back to the office the other day for deals in the pipeline. As far as listing and offers, Logan had eight in our system. Six of those were listings that he's made over the last year, one of them is a written offer that is to close in two weeks. I had many, many more. Twenty-five, to be exact, and if I look back over the last seven years, I think each year will be similar. And I'm happy to do that if you need it for any reason. But that woman will not be part of my business because Logan hasn't been part of my business in seven years."

Grant nodded. "That's fair. So I will tell Attorney Zsidai that you decline Logan's wish and Ms. Stigler's wish to be part of Price Realty."

"Yes, you can decline that request and further tell them about the five percent, or ten percent of fifty percent. Also, I ask that you please read through our incorporation documents and see if Logan even had the right to give off any percentage. I believe it had to be done by a proper procedure, through our corporate documents. I believe a written notice to the board, which are Logan and I, had to be made in writing, and shares had to be offered, voted on, and approved in the minutes of the meeting each year for that to pass. No share certificates were ever awarded. No written request to have shares given over were ever made, were ever voted on, and no certificates were given."

Grant nodded, "You're a smart woman Margo. I was going to get to that, but you beat me to it. So I'll look at that this week. In the meantime, I will ask Attorney Zsidai and Ms. Stigler to leave, and we'll tell them she will not be part of the business. Further, her proffered ten percent is only five percent."

"Yes, those are my wishes."

Grant stood and shook her hand, then Carley's. "It was nice meeting you, Carley."

"It was nice meeting you too, Mr. Parks."

He nodded. "If you two want to step out I will keep them

in the other conference room until you're gone so that you don't have to have an awkward run-in with her."

"Thank you, Grant. I do appreciate it and I'll wait for your call."

She left the building with Carley, and while the news was upsetting it wasn't as bad as she had thought. As she sat and listened to Attorney Zsidai and Grant, thoughts about the corporate documents came into her head. She felt better and better that Logan could go fuck himself wherever he was. He sure as hell wasn't in heaven. He wasn't getting his last wish or any wishes for that matter. And that fucking mistress of his could go to hell for all she cared. She was fighting mad. Even though she was fighting a dead man and his slut on the side.

13

Jace jogged down Main Street. He turned left onto his street, Classified Drive. He chuckled every time he saw the name. The house he'd purchased a couple of years ago was the former Governor's Mansion. It was his vacation home actually. The governor was shady, involved in too many illegal things, and the house sat empty for years when he slipped out into the night to hide from the FBI.

Jace had remodeled it, via Quinn and an interior designer, and it had been the perfect hideout for him hidden behind a forest of palm trees.

He could slip in and out, without anybody even knowing who owned the Governor's Mansion. These days that was a great feat for a small town. Not easy to do, especially since he owned a visible business.

Jogging up the front steps to his palatial looking home, he unlocked the door and stepped inside the cool air-conditioned home. Twisting the lock behind him, he enjoyed the cool air as it brushed his damp skin. He sauntered toward the kitchen at the back of the house. He made himself a large glass of ice water with electrolyte powder in it, watching the powder disappear as he stirred it.

He drank it down in between breaths, as he waited for his breathing to return to normal

He'd taken to jogging after the lunch hour every day. Unfortunately, it was the hottest part of the day, but he worked late nights and then slept in a bit later in the morning unless he had things on his mind. Then he worked his ass off all day. The last thing he wanted to do after he finished work was jog at one or two in the morning. So this had been his compromise - jog during the hottest part of the day, sweat like a pig, come back and replenish himself, and feel proud that he had gotten the jog in. That's where he was right now in today's journey.

Leaning with his back against the counter he thought about what he had to do yet today. A new band was playing from the neighboring town at the Sandbar tonight. Thank God he had Mason as his bartender, he was good. He was really good.

To try to keep his mind off the town council and what they would think of his business, which was what was keeping him awake at night, he'd asked Quinn to go with him, as well as the architect Quinn used to design the barracks for him. He'd come and answer questions. Just having those two people as a show of business acumen, he was going to do alright. That should have been enough to relieve his anxieties, but this was a big deal for him.

Slugging down the last of his electrolyte water, he trudged up the steps to his bedroom. He started the warm, not hot, water in the shower and began pulling out clean clothing for this evening at the Sandbar.

Jumping in the shower and letting the water cool his body, he closed his eyes and willed the water to wash away his anxieties. He was doing a good thing here. He was running a good business. Flashes of Margo shot through his head. What was it about her? Was it because she didn't like him, and he had this need to make everybody like him? Was that it?

Well, he wasn't gonna get tangled up in that. Why should he feel insecure about anything?

He finished his shower and dressed for the evening in a pair of khaki shorts, one of his bright-colored Hawaiian shirts, and his favorite brown leather sandals.

He jogged down the steps, stepped out of the front door, locked it behind him, and then sneaked through the palm trees to Sunset Beach Road, directly in front of Sarge's Sandbar.

The weather was beginning to cool, though it still needed to come down a little bit. As he stepped into the bar, Mason was behind it putting clean glasses away and setting up for the night. The Margarita fountain was full and ready to go. The Sandbar punch dispenser was filled and mixing their signature drink. The garnishes were cut - orange slices, lemons, limes, pineapple, and the cherry container was full.

"Are you all set Mason?" He looked over what still needed to be completed.

"Yep, getting there. The band is setting up outside."

"Good." He grinned and clapped his hands together. "Okay, let's get this party started."

Mason chuckled and Jace stepped outside to check the tables. Teresa, his longtime server, was straightening up chairs and raking the sand under the tables. He watched her work for a few moments and thought Quinn was right; having floating decks on the sand would be much better.

He was gonna do that for sure. It would also eliminate the sand coming into the bar every day.

People started filing in and taking a seat at their chosen table. The band began sound checks, and he happily set up Grace and Hanna's table. They had asked him to reserve their favorite table and he was happy to do it. He set up a special little centerpiece for them, a little bouquet he had delivered earlier in the day.

His friends supported him in everything he did. He wanted to support them as well. He kept himself busy until the band began playing, and the tables filled.

Hanna and Grace arrived, and he took them to their table. "Here you go, ladies. And just for you, special flowers."

"Oh!" Hanna exclaimed.

Grace grinned and leaned down to smell the flowers. When she stood up, she glanced around and saw none of the other tables had flowers.

"You are very thoughtful."

"I do what I can, ladies. What can I get for you?"

Grace smiled. "I'd like a glass of that red wine you have that I enjoy so much."

He nodded and chuckled. "A Merlot for Grace. And what can I get for you, Hanna?"

She smiled. "I'll take a Moscato, please."

He hustled to the bar to fill their orders.

When he delivered their drinks, Hanna said, "I invited Margo and her sister Carley here. They're going to sit with us tonight. I hope that's not a problem."

He froze slightly at Margo's name, but put a smile on his face. "Not a problem for me."

His heart beat a little faster when she mentioned Margo, and he hoped she was in a good mood. He didn't want to have another word match with her tonight. Certainly not while Hanna and Grace were here.

He began greeting guests, filling drink orders, and

running around when he saw the tall redhead come in by herself. She sat at a table on the opposite side of the beach from where his friends' wives were. But he couldn't help but notice that she was watching him everywhere he went.

After a while it became distracting. A feeling of unease crawled through him. Taking a deep breath, he made his way over to her table. "Hello there. What can I get you to drink?"

She smiled and shrugged her shoulders again. The word fake popped into his head. She was fake.

"I'll take..." She pursed her lips in a pouty fashion, "What is your special?"

"We have our Sandbar Punch which is a rum punch."

"That's what I want. The Sandbar Punch."

"Will do, coming right up." He sauntered back to the bar, stopping at tables along the way to say hello or check on drinks.

He ordered the Sandbar Punch from Mason, which was nothing more than adding ice to a glass, pouring the punch from the large dispenser, and adding the garnishes that were already made up.

He took a couple more drink orders while Mason prepared the Sandbar Punch then went back to get it.

He set the tropical drink in front of her. "Do you want to start a tab or pay right away?"

She smiled, lifted her right shoulder, and tossed a twenty-dollar bill on the table. "I'll pay you right away." She tugged on the bottom of his shirt and winked.

He took her money and hustled to the bar to make the change. When he returned with her change, he set it on the table and hurried to Hanna and Grace's table across the beach. As he approached, he saw Margo and her sister had arrived. And he smiled as brightly as he could. "Evening, ladies. Can I get you something to drink?"

Carley smiled, "I'd like that special drink with the pineapple in it."

He grinned, "That's our special, the Sandbar Punch."

Carley nodded. "I want one of those."

He chuckled and turned his eyes to Margo. She smiled, though it didn't look genuine, and he tried not to let that throw him. "I'd like a glass of Moscato, please."

"You got it, coming right up."

He hustled back to the bar to place their orders with Mason. Theresa was inside waiting for an order to be filled. "Hey, can you take care of the redhead at table twenty-two?"

She smiled, "Sure. Is she a little handsy?"

"Did you notice?"

"Oh yeah. I noticed. She's been watching you. When she isn't glaring at table six, that is."

He took a deep breath. Table six was Grace and Hanna's table. Hopefully, the redhead wasn't going to start something with either of them.

He hustled out to the table with their order. "Here you go, ladies."

He set their drinks in front of them and turned when a hand grabbed his shirt and spun him around. He was face to face with the redhead, and she had her arms wrapped around his neck. She was shimmying her body against his to the rhythm of the song the band was playing. He froze.

"Hey, I have to get to work."

"You can't have one sexy dance?" She purred.

"Ah, no. I have work to do."

He pulled his head back to look into her eyes. "What is going on here?"

"I just wanted to dance with you. You're so handsome."

Her voice was low as she channeled her Marilyn Monroe impersonation. A couple of the male clients whistled and yelled. "Got yourself a live one now, Jace."

No. He didn't want this reputation at all. He didn't want the Town Council to think this was some sort of a sleazy joint where he picked up women.

Another man he'd seen in here before brushed passed to go to a table. Jace grabbed the redhead's arms, lifted them off his shoulders, and put her arms on the other man's shoulders. "There you go, dance with him. He needs to dance a little."

The man laughed. "Well, thank you!"

Jace whisked by Hanna and Grace's table and grabbed his tray without stopping and hustled back to the safety of the bar.

He wasn't going to let anybody, certainly not a stranger, ruin his chances with the Town Council. Absolutely not.

14

Margo's jealousy rose to new highs. Just watching Sierra pawing at Jace, gyrating against him, moving with him. It irritated the shit out of her. She didn't understand why she felt twitchy. The need to crawl out of her skin was real. It was disgusting.

Carley leaned over to her. "It doesn't look like he's enjoying his time with her very much."

Margo turned to her sister. "I don't care what he does."

"No, I'm sure you don't," Carley said, "but he looks very uncomfortable. Margo, you have to admit that."

"Well, he can excuse himself. He doesn't have to take it."

Hanna looked over and smiled. "He owns a business. He doesn't want to make a scene. He's having a hard time here. Maybe I should go help him out."

Just then, she saw Jace grab each of Sierra's wrists with his hands, pull them off his shoulders, and put them on the shoulders of a man passing by. Jace nodded and said something to the man, who laughed, and then Jace strode away. He quickly came toward their table, grabbed the tray he had left there, and took off toward the bar.

Grace watched him hurry to the bar and frowned. "He's embarrassed. She embarrassed him. Who is that woman anyway?"

Margo met Grace's eyes. She let out a deep breath. "That's my late husband's mistress."

Both Grace and Hanna's jaws dropped open. Margo stared at them as they stared at her, none of them knowing exactly what to say.

Finally, Hanna said, "I'm so sorry, Margo. I had no idea."

"I didn't either until the day of the funeral," Margo responded.

Carley leaned forward. "While Logan was in the hospital, I noticed that his phone was chiming a lot, and I used his fingerprint to open the phone and saw all the texts from Sierra to Logan and back."

Grace gasped and put her hand over her mouth. "Oh my god, I can't believe that."

Carley nodded. "Seven years' worth, actually."

Hanna's mouth continued to drop open. Finally she said, "Are you fucking kidding me?"

Margo shook her head. "I've been reluctant to tell anybody. I have a fairly visible business and I didn't want people to associate it with something seedy and tawdry. And it's embarrassing."

Grace leaned forward. "It shouldn't be embarrassing for you, Margo. You've done nothing wrong."

"I know. But how could something like this go on for seven years and I was so completely oblivious to it."

Hanna, who sat to Margo's right, put her hand over Margo's and squeezed. "I know that feels embarrassing. Believe me, I do know. Someday you and I will have a glass of wine, and I'll tell you all the shady shit my ex, Isaac, did.

It's unbelievable, and I didn't know any of it was going on, but I didn't do anything wrong, and I was embarrassed, too. I completely understand why you feel that way, but you have absolutely nothing to be embarrassed about. Nothing."

Carley, who sat on her other side, nudged her lightly. "I told you. You don't have anything to worry about. Actually, you should let the whole town know what that fucker was up to."

Just then, Sierra laughed very loudly so everyone could hear, and the women all turned to look at her as she danced with the strange man that Jace had hoisted on her. That's when Margo noticed the necklace she was wearing. She touched her neck absently as she stared.

Carley said, "What's wrong?"

Margo shook her head slowly. "I think that's my necklace that she's wearing."

The women all turned again and stared at Sierra. When her dance partner twirled her in the sand, it glistened.

"Arc you sure?" Carley asked.

"I haven't looked at that necklace in years, to be honest with you. I think Logan bought it for me about five years ago, maybe longer. I can't remember. At the time, there was no occasion for it, and he took me completely by surprise. It looks exactly like mine unless he bought two at the same time, the dirty fucker."

"Hanna let out a groan. My god what men won't do."

Grace shook her head. "I don't know you guys. I'm so glad I have Sid now, but before that, I was sworn off of men myself."

Carley leaned forward. "When we get home, we're going to look for that necklace, and if it's not there we're gonna devise a plan."

"Yes, I agree with you."

And then Margo and Carley leaned forward conspiratorially to Hanna and Grace. "We had to go to the attorney's office today. Apparently, Logan also left Sierra Stigler, his mistress, ten percent of Price Realty. Hanna gasped again and put her hand over her mouth. "Un-fucking-believable."

"Well..." Margo said, "Actually, it's only ten percent of Logan's fifty percent. Luckily, we were equal partners, and I'm having Grant look that over to even make sure that that's the case. I don't think he can offer shares of the company without a sign-off, which would be both of us, and I did not sign anything, so we're checking into that."

"Oh my god. So is that why she's here?" Grace asked.

"I suppose," Margo responded. "She was at the attorney's office today when we went in, but Grant kept us in separate rooms. I didn't realize she was there until the end when he told Carley and to I to go ahead and leave and he would keep them in the other room until we were out of sight, so I didn't have to come face-to-face with her."

Grace leaned forward. "Does she know who you are?"

Just as she said that all the women turned toward Sierra, who was staring directly at Margo. She said, "I believe so."

At that moment, Jace was nearing as he delivered drinks to various tables. Hanna said, "You know Jace is a really good guy. He helps area veterans. Do you know all of his staff here are veterans? Most of them suffer from PTSD, or I think one of them has a hearing loss. There are a couple of others who have things that happened to them during the service. He helps them out. Sid and Quinn, too. That's why Quinn is remodeling the former army barracks in town here. He's turning them into housing for veterans, and I think Jace's bartender, Mason, is going to be one of the first tenants there or an owner if he decides to buy a condo."

Margo swallowed. "That's really nice of Quinn to do that, and that's very nice of Jace to help these men and women out."

She had to admit, he'd surprised her in a couple of ways today. Both were positive. And he was handsome.

15

Jace served drinks to several of the tables outside and noted as he glanced at Margo's table that the drinks were almost empty.

He hustled inside and asked Mason to mix up their drinks. There were three wines and one Sandbar Punch. He waited as Mason filled them up, noting the tables on the inside all had drinks.

They were doing a good job tonight of keeping everyone full. Mason set the drinks on his tray, and he told Mason, "This one's on the house from me, so note that in the till please."

"You got it, boss."

Jace carried the drinks outside and across the sand, careful to stay on the outside farthest away from the redhead.

He set the tray on the table. "Ladies these drinks are on the house."

He leaned in and served each lady their drink, took their empty glass away, and set them on the tray.

"Yay. Thank you," they each said.

He turned to leave and noted the redhead coming toward him.

Margo stood. "I'm going to excuse myself to the ladies' room."

He was a little bit of a pinch here. He turned toward Margo, wrapped his arms around her, and began dancing with her. She pulled away and her brows furrowed. The band changed the rhythm to a slow song, and he started swaying with her.

He liked the way she felt in his arms. He spun her around so she could see the redhead coming toward them and she instantly changed her demeanor.

"Looks like Sierra is coming for you."

"I'm not interested in Sierra. I am, however, very happy where I am right now."

She melted slightly in his arms. He felt her give in. Her arms slid up his chest and around his neck and they swayed as the song played.

"See this isn't so bad, is it?"

She chuckled. "No, no this is actually pretty nice."

"I'm glad you think so. I think it's pretty nice too."

His heartbeat increased as her scent wrapped around him. She smelled like citrus and cinnamon. The way she felt in his arms was like no other before her ever felt. He took a deep breath to keep his wits about him.

A tap on his shoulder had him turning to see the redhead standing there. "I'd like to cut in."

He shook his head. "Sorry, no cuts. I'm right where I want to be right now."

She landed a glare on Margo, who grinned a Cheshire cat grin. He didn't know what was going on between the two women, but he was going to take advantage of it. Not in a bad way, but it did get Margo to loosen up a little bit.

He swayed to the music and tightened his arms around her body. She was soft against him Her breasts pushed seductively against his chest and he had to keep sexy thoughts from other parts of his body.

Sierra stomped off and he enjoyed himself for a few minutes. Margo's arms stayed around his neck, her fingers slipped into his hair and kneaded his scalp. No one had ever done that before. He liked it. As in he wanted more of that.

As soon as the music began to die, he huffed out a deep breath. "Well, I'm sorry this is over. It was very enjoyable. Thank you for the dance, Margo."

"Yes, thank you. Thank you for the dance."

He leaned in, his lips next to her ear. "Maybe another one later on?"

She leaned back and looked into his eyes.

He grinned.

Her eyes were beautiful. Crisp blue surrounded by thick dark lashes. Her skin was tanned from their Florida sunshine and time spent outdoors. He hadn't seen her with makeup on before. She didn't need it to be beautiful, but the effect was magnetic. Her long, dark hair hung over her shoulders in waves.

She was a stunning woman. And he knew her to be smart and professional.

She finally responded. "Yeah, that would be nice."

"Say it like you mean it."

"I did."

"Nah, I think you can do it better."

"Do you want to dance with me or not?"

He threw his head back and laughed. "Yes, yes, I would like to dance with you again."

"Thank you." She smiled.

"Thank you for making me laugh."

"I'm sorry. I didn't mean to be so curt."

He smiled as he stared into her eyes. "No, no, no, no. I'm getting used to you being curt. You don't seem to like me all that much sometimes."

"It's not that. Maybe someday we'll talk about that."

"Okay, maybe someday. That would be good."

They finished their dance. He stepped away slightly and bobbed his head to her. "Thank you for this dance. I look forward to the next one."

He saw her swallow, her lips twitched at the corners. He waited for a snappy response, but she turned and headed toward the bar. He stopped at the table, picked up the tray of glasses, looked at Carley, and winked.

And she laughed and clapped her hands. The sister liked him. That was good. He'd work with that.

16

Margo was having a wonderful time. These women made her feel good. They didn't blame her. They understood. Hanna shared a little bit about what Isaac had been doing while they were married, and she realized they had something in common that other people would never understand.

Not that she was happy that Hanna had gone through that. She was a perfectly lovely woman. But she had someone in her life who knew what it felt like to be betrayed by someone. Someone that you loved. Jace came back to the table with another set of drinks, and she thought she'd better slow down. But he was so handsome. And he was attentive. And Hanna and Grace just couldn't say enough nice stuff about him. And Carley, she was a fan.

The music changed again to a slow, sultry song. Who was it that sang this song? She would have to try and remember. The singer had a low, slow, sultry voice. She'd have to think of it. Jace smiled. "Are you having a good time?"

"I am. These ladies are fantastic."

"That they are." He set her fresh drink in front of her and took the empty glass that she had pushed aside.

She said, "Would you like to dance?"

He bowed low and held his hand out toward the dance area. "After you."

She stood. Knowing the other women were watching, she decided not to turn and look at them. As she stepped toward the dance area, Jace grabbed her hand and held it in his. They walked together to the dance area. When was the last time Logan had held her hand? It had been years. She caught a quick glimpse of Sierra glaring at her as she turned slowly toward Jace and wrapped her arms around his neck. They danced slowly.

He pulled her body close to his. They hadn't danced this close before. But she liked it. She liked it a lot. And he smelled so good. Whatever aftershave he wore, it worked. It really worked for him. She could feel that he was toned and strong beneath his Hawaiian shirt. And he wasn't flirty like he had been before. And he didn't seem to like Sierra. That just made her all the more happy. She would like anyone who didn't like Sierra at this moment. They swayed to the music slowly.

And before thinking, she said, "Will you have dinner with me tomorrow night?"

He pulled his head back and looked at her for a long time. "Yeah. I'll have dinner with you."

"Thank you," she said.

He grinned, "How about if I pick you up at your house at, say, six o'clock?"

"Yes. I'd like that."

"Okay, six it is."

He laid his cheek next to the side of her head. They

swayed to the song standing incredibly close, their bodies touching almost everywhere.

She lifted her face to stare into his eyes. "Logan had a seven-year affair with Sierra."

His brows rose as he stared into her eyes. "I'm very sorry. He shouldn't have done that. I can't imagine how anyone would want to hurt you, Margo."

She felt brave now. Maybe it was the wine. Or her company. "Not only that, but he changed his will a couple of years ago and gave her ten percent of my real estate company."

Jace stared into her eyes for a long time. Oh, she liked looking at his. They were sexy. And he stared at her fully. He didn't look away. He continued to give her his attention. After a few moments, he asked her softly, "How does that make you feel?"

She opened her mouth to say something but wasn't really quite sure what to say. No one had asked her how she felt about anything in a long time. Her heartbeat sped up, and she took a couple of deep breaths.

She shook her head quickly as if to try and shake out cobwebs. Then she responded, "It makes me mad. It makes me sad that he wanted to betray me like that. It makes me sad that we really haven't had a marriage in seven years, and I was completely unaware of it. Though now as I look back, I see it. I see it all. I just buried myself in work as our marriage became routine and Logan began traveling more. And I feel mad that he will never get my swift. Hard. Kick. Right in the nuts."

Jace stared into her eyes for a long time. Then he burst out laughing. He threw his head back and she looked at his tanned handsome neck and his jaw. And when he tilted his head down, his smile was still there, and she couldn't stop staring at him. His tanned face, framed by his short dark hair, was appealing. A slight stubble had grown on his jaw and chin throughout the day, which only added to the darkness of his tone. He was incredibly handsome. Swaying with him to the music, she could feel the firmness of his body. He was strong, she felt it in the way he held her. But he was attentive in a way she hadn't remembered Logan, or anyone actually, being before.

"Now that's a good one. But, as a guy - ouch!"

Her smile grew slightly as she stared into his handsome eyes. "Well, I need to get the anger out there. If he were standing in front of me right now, I'd probably not do that. But, when I'm sitting still and thinking, that's what I think about."

He nodded slowly. His eyes scanned the area quickly. He was working. And he was the owner here. The responsibility was all his and she admired his commitment to his business. "I can understand that. Do you have any idea what it will take for you to get over the anger?"

She frowned. "No."

He shrugged his left shoulder. "Fair enough."

He guided her into a simple turn, which wasn't easy on the sand. She'd kicked her shoes off a while ago, finding the curling of her toes in the sand comforting. Like one of those little Zen gardens where you had the tiny rake and could make shapes in the sand. But, instead, she curled her toes and relaxed them. Dancing now with Jace, the sand on her feet was warm. He spun them slowly once more, and then they slowed and swayed. He was a good dancer, and she hadn't danced with a man in a long time. Actually, a very long time. Maybe five years ago, when she and Logan had attended the wedding of a friend in Tampa.

"You're a good dancer," she absently whispered.

He chuckled. "I don't know about that. I love music, though. There's something about allowing the music to seep in. Adding a beautiful woman in my arms while the music is seeping in is a bonus. I don't get a lot of time to dance, as you can imagine."

"You've managed it a few times tonight."

He pulled his head back slightly and looked into her eyes. "Tonight is a special night."

"Why is it so special?" She did want to know, though she was worried about his response for some strange reason.

His smile was pure sexiness. If there was a picture in the dictionary for sexy, this would be it. "The weather is perfect. The music is wonderful. Business is thriving and going to be expanding." He halted briefly, then softly added, "and I have the most beautiful woman in town in my arms."

"I'll bet you say that to all the girls."

He shook his head. "I don't. I have never said it to anyone, actually."

She shook her head. When he flirted, it set off warning bells in her head. "Right."

"I'm hurt you don't believe me."

"I'm not sure my trust levels are at a point to trust many people these days."

"Fair enough. Do you trust me to kick this dance up a notch?"

She hesitated. The band easily shifted to an upbeat tempo, and Jace's arms tightened around her. He commanded her movements gently but firmly as they skirted the entire area in front of the stage. They moved with such ease she felt as though she were floating. Each turn and step felt effortless, and he never let her go. When the music stopped, he stepped away slightly and bowed. "That was remarkable. And fun. Thank you, Margo Price for such an energetic interlude in my schedule."

Her heart skipped a beat. Man, he was something. "You're welcome. Thank you for spending some of your precious time with one of your customers."

He chuckled and shook his head. "You are so much more than a mere customer."

He took her hand and led her to her table. Her friends stared at her, and finally, Carley said, "You two were on fire out there. We so enjoyed watching you two dance with each other. I didn't know you knew how to dance like that."

"I don't. Didn't. I mean it was all Jace."

He grinned and shook his head. "You don't give yourself enough credit."

A server rushed toward Jace at that moment, "Jace. We have an issue in the kitchen."

He turned to her and nodded once. "Later. Gotta go."

17

Jace rushed into the kitchen as the chef, Marco, growled.

"What's going on?"

"Stove stopped working. I've got orders coming out of my ass and no stove."

"Good lord, I hope they aren't flying out of your ass. Let me take a look."

He reached behind and turned the gas off. He then turned it back on and tried the igniter. He messed with a few things and finally got the stove to light. "Let's get through tonight. I'll call in the morning for repair. It seems like a burp in the gas line."

Marco immediately turned to one of the prep assistants. "Back up. Start plating." And things returned to the hurried normal of the day.

Jace strode around the tables, ensuring everyone had drinks, picked up dirty dishes, and generally chatted with customers. His eyes never strayed far from the table in the corner with the gorgeous blue-eyed realtor.

He shook his head to dislodge the thoughts. He hadn't

truly been enamored with a particular woman in...what was it? Years. He'd been kicking around, dealing with PTSD and what to do with his life. He'd grown a beard and let his hair grow, then shaved it all off. Found a job and quit said job. Then he came here. While he enjoyed looking at beautiful women, what man didn't? It had stayed just that way...great to look at. But Margo, he found himself wanting to be near her. Talk to her. Stare into her eyes.

He replaced a few drinks, checked with Marco to make sure the stove was still working, and he wasn't losing his cool, then sauntered toward Margo.

"Do you ladies need a refill?"

Carley giggled and he made a mental note to check on how they'd get home. All the women were giggling and showing signs they'd drank too much to drive.

Carley looked up at him. "Do you have Uber here?"

He chuckled. "Yeah, we have Uber."

She smiled. She and Margo looked similar, but Margo, in his opinion, was prettier.

"I want another drink. This one's on me." Carley giggled.

Grace nodded. "I'll take one on Carley."

Hanna held up her glass. "Me too."

He turned his head to Margo and saw her watching him. He lifted his brows, and she smiled a soft, mesmerizing smile. "I'll take one more. Then I'm done."

"Coming up."

Sid and Quinn strode toward the table, the grins on their faces caused him to grin. Quinn leaned down and kissed the top of Hanna's head. "Got your hands full here, Jace?"

Jace chuckled. "Nah. It's all good. You guys want a drink? The ladies just ordered another one."

Sid nodded. "Yep, not gonna sit here without one."

Jace chuckled. "I'll be right back."

He hustled off to order up the drinks and just before he stepped into the bar Sierra came out of nowhere. "I haven't seen you much tonight," she purred.

"Ahh." He took a breath. "No, it's a busy night here. Guests come first."

"Unless you're dancing with one of them." Her tone had changed slightly, and warning bells went off in his head. This one is a troublemaker.

"Unless that," he clipped.

Mason slid the tray of drinks across the bar to him and tilted his head slightly toward the redhead. Jace, grateful to have someone like him with intuition simply nodded once. Sierra looked the drinks over on his tray, she turned to look at a couple of them and grinned. "Quite the group out there."

"That it is."

He picked up the tray to leave and Sierra stopped him by standing in front of him. Before he could say anything, Mason raised his voice to be heard over the speakers filling the bar with the sounds of the band outside. "Can I buy you a drink on the house?"

Sierra's eyes glared into his for a moment, then shifted to Mason's. "Sure." She sauntered toward Mason, and Jace hurried outside without a backward glance.

He set the tray of drinks on the table, then one by one, delivered the drinks to his friends and their significant others, and Margo and Carly. As soon as he set Margo's drink down, her lips parted and formed a seductive smile. "Thanks," she mouthed.

That sent a spiral of emotion from his neck to his crotch. She'd loosened up this evening and it was beguiling to watch her. Sierra exited the bar and Jace took a deep breath. He nodded to Margo and held his hand out to her.

"Care to twirl around on the dance floor, so to speak, once more?"

Her smile grew. "Yes, I'd love that."

The women at the table all clapped and he hurriedly took Margo's hand in his and led her to the area in front of the stage.

He turned to her and wrapped her body in his arms and a feeling came over him he'd never had before. Comfort? Longing? Desire? He'd had desire before, but this was different.

Sierra sauntered passed them, letting her eyes shoot daggers toward Margo and Margo took a deep breath and let it out.

He leaned his head closer to hers. "In case you haven't noticed, Sierra is a gold digger. Now I don't know this for a fact, but she isn't someone grieving for Logan, or anyone, she claimed to love. She's been handsy with me and a bit over-the-top, bold and seductive. She came into the sandbar this morning with some pudgy little man. They had lunch and the entire time she flirted with me. And you want to know what I thought?"

Margo shook her head. "What did you think?"

He said, "I thought that must be what Margo thinks of me when she sees me flirting. I didn't think what I was doing was flirting. I love this place, Margo. I love what I'm doing. It's the first time since..." he swallowed. "It's the first time since I came home from the service that I have felt like I found my calling. I've kicked around in jobs, and I've tended bar here and there. I didn't want to do this, and I didn't want to do that, and basically my PTSD kept me from doing anything regular. I would have attacks, and if the pressure got too high, I couldn't take it, and it caused me to flounder. Then Quinn asked me a couple of years ago to come down here. He said, 'Come down. Stay. You can stay with me. You can kick about all you want to. You can look for a job or not. But come.' So I did because I didn't really have anything to lose. So I came down here, and the first night Quinn and I came to this bar. It didn't look like this then. It was just a little hole-in-the-wall bar. It was dirty, but it was the only one on the beach. The old guy behind the bar was slow, making me practically crawl out of my skin because I saw all the lost opportunities. He wasn't getting people their drinks on time, and they would get frustrated and leave. He was slow. The place was dirty. There were so many things that could be improved without money. It was just getting someone competent behind the bar, and I don't know, maybe the old man didn't have the money, but I offered. I called him over to Quinn and me and said, 'I'd like to tend bar here.' He looked at me and he laughed. Then he glanced at Quinn and Quinn said, 'He's good people man. He's good people.' The old guy knew Quinn pretty well and trusted him, so the old guy said, 'Okay, well why don't you come in tomorrow at eight o'clock and help me get things set up.' So I was here the next morning. I helped him set up. I cleaned up behind the back bar. I got beer coolers filled and made sure the taps were clean. Something that hadn't been done in a while, and when the first customers walked in, I greeted the pants off them. I was friendly. I was happy. I was serving them drinks, and the till kept going cha-ching, cha-ching, cha-ching. It didn't take long before the locals started bringing their friends in, and the bar started filling up, and the old man told me, 'You're doing all right, kid. Doing all right.' It was maybe a couple months later he came in one day and said, 'You know, watching you these past couple of months, I realize where I was lacking. I don't have it anymore. So why don't you buy the bar from me?' I didn't have to think about it. I said, 'yes.' I had some money stashed. Actually, I wasn't really living anywhere in particular so I had money stashed from the service and from my deployment pay and from my parents when they passed. I bought the bar, paid cash and then I dug in. I started cleaning. I started fixing things up. It doesn't hurt that my best friend, one of my best friends, owns a construction company. He sent a crew in, and we spent a weekend cleaning this place up. Then the business rolled in, and it got busier and busier, and I added a little bit here and I added a little bit there. And basically Margo, when I am telling women I think they're beautiful or they look good or I smile and greet people, it's because I love it here. I love being the host. I love greeting customers. I love that they want to come here. I didn't look at it as flirting, but you kind of made me think that maybe I need to pull back a little bit."

She shook her head. "No, Jace, no I didn't mean that. I don't want you to feel bad. You are good at what you do. I've been watching you tonight. You're just talking to people. You're making them feel good. Making them feel welcome. That's something that most businesses don't do anymore. You make me want to be here. You make me want to stay here. You've got music going and the atmosphere is, well Sierra aside, the atmosphere is welcoming and happy and we're on the beach no less."

He grinned. " I see that you know what I mean."

"I do and I'm sorry I was terse with you earlier. I had just come off the news of Logan cheating on me and I thought all men were cheats and liars."

He shook his head. "Honey, I'm not a cheat and I'm not a liar. Those are qualities I don't like in other humans, and I will never have them in myself. Ask Sid and Quinn if you don't believe me. They're my best friends. We've spent years together. We spent a horrible time in the service together. Deployed, shot at, wondering if we were gonna make it home from each mission. But I have never lied, and I don't cheat."

She took a deep breath, and he watched her process his words.

She smiled sweetly, "Can we start over?"

He laughed. "I'd love that. Let's start over." He stepped back and held his hand out to her. She lay her hand in his and he smiled. "My name is Jace Marriott. I'm the owner of this fine establishment. Welcome to Sarge's Sandbar. The nicest place in the State of Florida."

She smiled, and it was spectacular. It reached her eyes. She looked genuinely happy. "My name is Margo Price, and I'm a real estate agent. I'm happy to meet you, Jace Marriott."

They shared a laugh, and he wrapped his arms around her once more and spun them in the sand.

He felt a tap on his shoulder and dread filled his gut. He looked into Margot's eyes, which stared into his. She raised her eyebrows in the air, and he grinned.

He slowly turned his head to see Sierra standing there. "Mind if I cut in?"

He nodded. "Yes, I do mind. I'm dancing with the most beautiful woman in the place right now and that's where I'll stay. Thank you though."

He twisted to spin Margot away from Sierra and she laughed out loud. A quick glance at Sierra saw her stomping off looking pissed. While he wasn't one to chase away customers, he was happy to chase this one away.

18

Margo sighed when she and Carley arrived at her place. They'd been sensible and let Sid and Grace drive them home. She'd have to go pick up her car in the morning. Sure, she'd had a few drinks. So what. It was just what she needed to let go of some of the tension. And, dammit, Jace made her feel special. Beautiful. Desirable.

My god, how long had it been since she'd really and truly felt that way?

She sat on the sofa and kicked her sandals off. Carley sat in a chair across from her and toed her sandals off. Carley took a deep breath and let it out slowly. She pulled her phone from her purse and scrolled a bit.

Margo frowned. "If you're going to ignore me, I'm going to bed."

"I'm not ignoring you. I wanted to show you a couple of pictures." She found what she'd been looking for and came to sit next to her on the sofa. She held her phone in front of Margo and grinned. "Look."

She'd taken a picture of her and Jace dancing. They were

smiling at each other, and she had her arms around Jace's neck. His arms were wrapped around her, and the muscles in his arms stood out to her. She'd felt that strength. Looking at him now, though, he was s-e-x-y.

"Wow," she whispered.

"I know. You too look so good together. I couldn't resist taking the pictures."

"Pictures? How many did you take?"

"Scroll."

She scrolled to the next picture which was Jace's head thrown back laughing. It was incredible.

The next picture was them walking to the dance area hand in hand. He was easily ten inches or so taller than her. Her hair managed to keep some of its wave despite the humidity. She smiled as she stared.

Scrolling to the next picture was one of Jace whispering in her ear or chatting with her. She remembered him telling her he didn't think of himself as a flirt. He was happy. Why had she not recognized that? Happiness and flirting were not the same thing.

She scrolled once more and stared at the two of them looking at each other, she was telling him something.

Carley leaned in, "That's my favorite picture."

"Really? It's not the best one."

Carley giggled. "I know, but look over your shoulder."

She pulled the phone closer and looked. Sierra could be seen just behind her.

"Blow the picture up and look at her face."

With her thumb and forefinger, she stretched the picture and looked at Sierra's face. Margo grinned. "If looks could kill."

Carley laughed and clapped her hands. "That's what I

thought." She sat back and rested her head on the sofa. "Logan was a dumbass."

Margo forwarded the pictures to her phone, then handed it back to Carley. She leaned back with her head on the sofa, too, and stared up at the ceiling with her sister. "I agree."

Carley chuckled and took Margo's hand in hers. They sat that way for a while and then she said, "Are we looking for your necklace tonight or tomorrow?"

"Tonight. I'll end up waking up about two in the morning otherwise, and start thinking about it."

Carly sat up with a sigh. "Okay. Let's go do it."

"You don't have to help me. You can get some rest if you like."

"Nope. I'm here with you and for you. Let's go."

Margo nodded. She stood, and they walked together down the hall to the master bedroom. Margo's jewelry box was built into the closet when she and Logan built this house. It was something that she'd always wanted and was so excited to have. She lifted the top of the jewelry box, pulled out the boxes that were inside, and handed them to Carley. Any nice piece of jewelry she had gotten she kept in its box and put it away for safekeeping. She opened the drawers and pulled out boxes. Carly took them out and laid them on the bed. Once all of them were on the bed, they sat on the edge and opened the lid of each box. Her necklace box was not there.

Carley said, "I don't even know what to think. Why would he do that? That makes no sense. He could have just bought her a new necklace."

Margo shook her head. She scraped her fingers through her hair and stretched her back. The deeper we get into this whole ridiculous situation the more questions I have. None of it makes sense. None of it. I can't even imagine why he would come home here, have dinner with me, talk about business, and act like nothing was wrong while he was having an affair. I can't imagine that he took his estate planning folder out of the safe, had his will changed two years ago, and still had dinner with me and acted like nothing was wrong. Like everything was fine. We weren't lovey-dovey anymore. No. And you know, I can't even remember the last time we had sex, but he certainly wasn't angry toward me. We didn't have animosity. I simply don't understand it. And now the necklace."

Margo looked across the bed at all the jewelry. Over the years, she acquired a beautiful collection of necklaces, earrings, and bracelets. The weird thing was she seldom wore any of it anymore. When she was younger, she thought she wanted the jewels. But the Florida heat normally made her sweat, and she didn't like to wear jewelry that was hanging on her neck when it was so hot. Unless it was for a special occasion.

Carley stood. "I don't understand any of it either, Margo. It's the weirdest damn thing, isn't it?"

"It is, and now I don't even know how I'll ever get the answers I want."

"We could go to a...what do they call them? A medium and have a seance? We could ask that fucker."

Margo chuckled. "If he's this much of a coward he won't even show up dead."

She looked at her sister and they both laughed. "I mean what more could you do?"

She laughed. Carley laughed, and then they laughed harder together, and it felt good to laugh. She shook her head. "I didn't even know if I could laugh, but it just seems to be so stupid, and I can't stop thinking about how much like a prank this is. Like I'm waiting for this fucker to come back and say, 'Gotcha!'"

"That's what I was thinking too."

Margo paced across the floor a couple of times, and then she froze. "Oh my god, I had this all insured." She ran to her closet, knelt, and opened the safe. She pulled some paperwork out of the safe and found the envelope she was looking for. She brought it out to the bedroom and opened it up.

"Carley, I had that necklace insured."

They looked through the paperwork and found the document for the diamond necklace that Logan had given her. She had to take pictures of it. She had the information on the size, the carat weight, and the gold weight of the necklace. It was all included in the insurance papers. It was all there.

"He didn't give her this. He forgot about this."

Carley clapped her hands. "This is fantastic. You can turn this into the insurance company and put that little bitch in jail for theft."

"That's certainly an idea and one that I'm going to think about for a little while. But don't tell anybody about this just yet. I want to think on it long and hard before I put things into motion like that."

"I get it, but Margo this is great. This is...this is fantastic. You can at least threaten her with it. Watch her smug face fall."

"Right. Right, I can certainly do that. By the way..." she halted and waited for Carley to turn and look at her. "I asked Jace Marriott out on a date tomorrow night."

Carly's smile grew large, and she got up and ran to her sister and hugged her tight. "I'm so proud of you Margo. I am so proud of you. And whew he's a hottie."

19

Jace sat at his kitchen table reading over the paperwork he was emailed from the title company. He was mostly checking his name, spelling, his address, the address of the thrift store, and the totals. The closing costs were nil. He wasn't having an inspection. He wasn't having a title policy issued. He wasn't having anything done because he was bulldozing the place the second he could. It all looked good to him. The selling price was the same and correct.

All he had to pay for was the deed and the title company's fee. The seller had to pay Margo's fee, which he was happy about. She was doing a pretty good job. She had emailed him this morning forwarding the title company paperwork and told him to look it over. *Call me when you're finished.* That last little sentence gave him a thrill. Call me when you're finished.

At just after eight o'clock, he called his bank to double-check that they were ready to wire the money over on Friday. They agreed they were ready to do that. They just needed the wiring information from the title company. He could get that to them.

And then he called Margo. He'd be lying if he said he wasn't excited to talk with her. As a matter of fact, the second he heard her soft, low sexy voice greet him with, "Hello" chills ran up the back of his neck.

"Good morning."

"Good morning," she replied.

"So I just read through the paperwork you forwarded from the title company. Thank you. I've contacted my bank. They're ready to wire the funds. They just need the wire transfer information."

"Okay, I'll make sure they get that this afternoon. Tomorrow at the latest."

"Good, thank you. I'll wait to hear from you about that. If you would just let me know when the title company has contacted the bank with that information, I'd appreciate it."

"Will do. I'll just ask the title company to take care of it. Sometimes, numbers can get transposed when they go through too many hands, so I usually let them do their job and take care of that. Just email me your bank's name, the phone number, and who you deal with there, and we can have the title company take care of the rest from there. They'll copy you and me on the email."

He chuckled. "Will do. I like letting someone else do their job."

She laughed. "Me too. It's kind of nice, isn't it? Not having to do everything."

"That it is." He was silent for a moment, his stomach tightened. He let out a breath and said, "Margo, I know we have a date tonight. Did you want to keep it?"

"Of course. Why wouldn't I want to keep it?"

He shrugged though no one could see it. "I thought maybe you asked me because Sierra was there."

She let out a long breath. "I'll admit it prompted the question at first, but as the night wore on, I became more and more excited about our date."

He smiled so big his cheeks stretched. "Good. I've been looking forward to it. I thought we'd go somewhere outside of Blossom Springs so we could both just sit and get to know each other. With both of us owning businesses in town, it's kind of hard not to know someone wherever we go."

"That's a fact. I like that idea. Thank you for thinking of it."

"Of course. So..." He hesitated, then decided to go for it. "Did you find the necklace?"

She huffed. "No."

"Oh..." he tsked. "Shit. I'm sorry."

"Well as I've told my sister every time a new issue comes up, or a new surprise presents itself with this whole ridiculous situation, it helps me get over the grief that much easier. I'll tell you I had no idea I was sharing my house with such a lying piece of shit. No idea. It's like he was a complete stranger."

"Yeah, I can't imagine how that must feel, and I am sorry for that Margo. You don't deserve it."

"Well, thank you. I do appreciate that."

"Okay, well, I'll see you at six o'clock tonight. I'll pick you up. We'll just do casual. How about that?"

She chuckled, and it sounded good. "Casual sounds great. I can't wait. Thank you. Talk to you later. Bye."

He hung up the phone, and he wished he could sit and talk with her. He wanted to know more about her. Why did she like real estate? What were all the things that he wanted to know about her? Mostly, what he knew right now was that he thought she was stunning and smart, and her poise through all of this turmoil, as he looked at it now, the few terse words she had spoken to him were nothing compared to what he would have done had the shoe been on the other foot. She was handling this far too gracefully. But it spoke about her class and her demeanor. And he wanted to get to know her so much better.

20

Margo got a bit of work done at the office, mostly for Jace's closing, but she had some customers who had called, and she needed to take care of certain closing things. Make sure the title companies were lined up, schedule closings, and then she needed to touch base once again with the closing that Logan had in the pipeline that was to close in two weeks.

She arrived home just before noon, and she was tired. She hadn't slept much last night. Irritation over the necklace and what to do about it, and Logan and his lying and cheating and now stealing, wouldn't let her sleep. She thought before she went out for her date with Jace, she should certainly take a nap. And she had Carley at her house, so she wanted to get home and spend some time with her sister. She wasn't going to be there very long. After all, she had her own home to get to and a boyfriend waiting for her.

As soon as she walked into the door, the house smelled freshly cleaned. Music played softly through the built-in speakers. She glanced around and everything was in its place, the vacuum marks stood out on the white carpeting and the oven timer sounded from the kitchen. Such a welcome feeling.

She set her briefcase on the floor near the entertainment center where she always kept it and moved toward the kitchen. Carley pulled a fresh sheet of cookies from the oven as she entered.

"Hi. I thought I'd try my hand at this chocolate chip cookie recipe I found. I'm sure they aren't Hanna quality, but I like having a cookie with my coffee in the morning."

"They smell wonderful."

Carley smiled. "Sit." She pointed to the counter opposite her where the bar stools were.

Carley pulled a plate from the cupboard, scooped a fresh hot cookie straight from the sheet, and laid the cookie on it. "Milk?" She asked.

"Ah...sure." Margo smiled.

Carley fussed over her a moment and poured them each a glass of milk.

Then it dawned on her. When was the last time she walked into this house and felt welcomed to be home? It seemed like she had grown accustomed to the fact that she was supposed to be here, walk into the house, and decide what she had to do first, then second. Was Logan going to be home? Supper needed to be made. Laundry needed to be done. Dust. Vacuum. Mow the lawn. All of it had fallen to her over the years. To be honest, Logan had never made her feel welcome. His conversations and questions were always, did you get any listings today? Did you write any offers? When's the next closing on your schedule? Mine is this day. Things were business-y. Is that all they ever had was a business relationship?

It puzzled her that she'd never noticed it, but now that

the thought entered her head, she didn't see it leaving anytime soon.

Carley lifted her glass of milk and held it between them. Margo grinned and picked up hers. They clinked their glasses together, and Carley grinned. "Welcome home. I'm making lunch. It'll be finished soon. Crock-Pot stew."

"Where did you learn to make that?"

"Well, I found this recipe this morning as I was looking through the internet."

"Oh dear, I'm your guinea pig recipe taster?"

"Well, actually, it sounded good, and I've been taste testing a little bit as I've been making it. It's pretty good, Margo. I think you're gonna like it. I also am making puff pastry spinach, mushroom, bacon bites, and I'm making a little sauce that you can dip them into if you like."

"That sounds really good actually."

"I didn't want to make anything with cabbage, or you know that would make you bloat for your date tonight. No sense in having a gassy belly."

"Well, thank you for that. That would be embarrassing, wouldn't it? To have my stomach roiling and rumbling."

"It would."

Margo looked into her glass and moved it around in small circles on the counter. The milk swirled around, and she watched the patterns it made. "Are you sure this isn't too soon for me, Carley?"

"I'm certain it isn't too soon. When you think about it now, you haven't really been married to Logan for a long time. His formality of actually dying, in some ways, did you a favor. He set you free, Margo. You're free now to have a life."

She stared at her sister for a minute. She was pretty. She wore her hair a bit shorter than Margo did, but it was the same dark color as their father's. Same blue eyes. Carley had her mom's cute little nose, but otherwise, they were similar.

"I've never thought of it that way."

"Well, start thinking about it that way. He did you no favors by keeping you in this marriage. It's like he wanted his cake and to eat it too."

"Well, more like a cash cow, I was the one bringing in all the money."

"Well, there may be that since we don't know what the dumbass was thinking, all we can do is speculate, and that probably doesn't do any of us very much good. So, let's not speculate. How about that?"

Carley picked up her cooling cookie and took a bite. She grinned. "It's good."

Margo bit into hers and agreed. "You did a good job with these."

Margo took another bite, sipped her milk, and finished her cookie. "Carley, you're spoiling me. What am I gonna do when you go home?"

Carley flinched and Margo paused. "Is everything okay at home with you?"

"Well, I didn't want to bother you before since you've been going through so much. But Don and I have broken up."

"When did that happen?"

"It happened about a month ago, and I waited for a while to tell anybody because, well, I was processing it myself. And then Logan got sick, and I came here, and it was a nice reprieve not have to deal with the daily arguments and sniping at each other, which seemed to be the case. And when I went back after the funeral, I realized I didn't want to be there. I came back here partly...mostly, to help you through all of this, but also to give myself some space and decide what I want to do."

"Oh my god, honey, I didn't know."

Margo ran around the counter and hugged her sister. She hugged her tight. "I wish you would have let me know about this. All this time I've been blabbing on and on, and the focus was on me. We should have been focusing on you."

Carley mumbled, "No, we should have been focusing on both of us, I guess, but I wasn't sure I wanted to say anything just yet."

Margo pulled back and looked her sister in the eye. "All right, so are you moving out or did he move out?"

"Well, I think I'm going to move out. I don't want to be in that house anymore. I know we bought it together, but he'll have to buy me out. I've already spoken to Grant Park. Actually, I called him today while you were at the office to see if he could guide me through forcing Don to sell the house and giving me my share of the equity, which will get me started somewhere else."

"Here, let it be here. Come here. Move here by me. We'll be close."

Carley smiled. "That's kind of what I was thinking. But I didn't want you to feel burdened with me being underfoot."

"You're not underfoot. Oh my god, Carley, come and live here. Stay here with me. You have your own room. You have your own bathroom. Do what you want to do until you either find another job or see if you can work remotely from your current job or whatever you decide to do. But come here. Live with me."

Carley smiled. "Let me just say this. That sounds great. I love being with you, and I'm absolutely going to think about it, but I also don't want to jump into a relationship where I'm dependent on someone else. So let me just give it some good thought, okay?"

"Deal. That's a deal."

Carley nodded. "Okay, so now let's get you fed, and then you should take a nap before you have to get ready for your date tonight. And I want you to think about your date tonight and let him admire you and show you what a real man is like because I think he's the real deal, Margo."

Margo wore a white skort and a soft blue sleeveless blouse. She'd curled her hair and played with it in the mirror. Up or down? The temperature would begin to cool in about an hour, but right now, it was still in the high eighties.

"You look gorgeous either way."

Carley entered the bathroom and sat on the little stool against the wall near the window.

"I was worried about the heat. He said casual but I'm not sure if we'll be inside or outside."

Carley lifted and dropped her right shoulder. "Then wear it up and pull it down when the sun goes down."

Margo gathered her hair together at the nape of her neck and twisted it. She pulled it up and secured it with a pretty clip, letting the waves on the long end fall over the twist in waves.

Margo turned toward Carley and held her hands out to the sides.

Carley grinned. "Perfect."

"Thank you." Margo took a deep breath and let it out slowly. "What are you going to do while I'm out?"

"I'm going to take a bath and read a book. Maybe have a glass of wine."

"Okay." Margo swallowed, and Carley leaned forward. "Remember back in the day when you enjoyed life? As in, just living? Waking up excited about what the new day would bring."

"Of course."

"Do you?"

Margo opened her mouth and closed it. Did she? She frowned slightly.

Carley stood and hugged her. Stepping back, she looked into her eyes. "Do that again. Last night, you enjoyed dancing with Jace. The pictures don't lie. Enjoy spending time with a handsome man and enjoy that he treats you special."

"Does he? Treat me special?"

"He held your hand as you walked to the dance area. He told Sierra to buzz off. He looks at you like you're the most beautiful woman on the planet. Enjoy that. And treat him nice too."

The doorbell rang and Margo's hands pressed against her belly. Carley shook her head. "Get yourself calmed down, and I'll go let him in."

Margo turned to look at herself one more time. She looked good tonight. The nap sure helped. Her hair looked good and the gaunt look she'd had while Logan was in the hospital was gone. She looked healthy.

Stepping out to the hallway, she padded toward the front door as she heard Carley and Jace chatting.

"Would you like something to drink?"

"No, thank you. I'm driving and I have a bottle of water in the truck. Besides, I don't drink much."

"But you make a living selling drinks."

Jace laughed and the sound was beautiful. Deep, rich, and real. "Ah, yes, it's best not to drink the profits."

Carley laughed. "Good point."

Margo stepped into the room. Jace looked fantastic. Handsome in his grey three-button placket shirt and khaki shorts. His legs were tanned from days in the sun serving guests. His broad shoulders stretched the soft cotton shirt in the best way. His eyes landed on hers, and her tummy fluttered.

"You look gorgeous as always, Margo."

She was speechless for a moment. "Thank you. You are as handsome as ever."

He grinned. "Looks like we should go out and enjoy it."

Margo glanced at Carley. She hugged her and whispered. "Remember what that feels like right there. The flutter in your belly and the goosebumps on your arms."

21

Jace drove them out of town. He felt strongly about being able to spend some time alone. In the beginning, they didn't really like each other all that much or, at least, she didn't like him. It was all a misunderstanding, though. He hoped after last night, he'd managed to get that cleared up. He wasn't a player, he'd never been a player. Of course, he was divorced, and he had an ex who didn't understand or want to understand PTSD. If he were being honest, which he always liked to be, not being able to hold a job when he first came back from Iraq, being scared and confused all the time, and not even understanding PTSD himself, he probably wasn't a good husband. It just put too much stress on the relationship, but it was after that divorce that he finally decided to seek counseling. He'd go for a while. It would feel too personal, too hard to change, and then he'd stop going, only to realize after a time that it was actually kind of helping. So he'd looked up his counselor, started making more appointments, and joined groups to help. Oddly, or maybe not, it was Quinn and Sid who were the biggest help. He'd call one or both of them.

Sometimes, they managed group calls, and he talked to them about something that scared him that day or caused him to have a panic attack. When Sid confided that he had the same thing, they really started talking, and then Quinn admitted that there were times when he struggled, too. These three friends, who had been together through some of the toughest times, learned that they were each other's support more than anything else. Then he started feeling better. As he started feeling better, he looked for jobs that he thought he would like to do. He'd been somewhat of a mechanic in the military. Not as good as Sid, and he wouldn't even try. Sid could fix anything. But Jace sort of liked being with people.

Mostly, what he liked was seeing people happy. So that took out counseling, but when he came down to Blossom Springs at Quinn's urging and started working at this little hole-in-the-wall bar on the beach, he found what he was looking for. He hadn't had an actual PTSD attack since he'd been down here in Blossom Springs. That felt pretty damn good. He was sort of a counselor but in his own way.

He said, "I thought we'd go to Spring Harbor. There's a neat little restaurant there called The Clamshell that I've been hearing an awful lot about. Customers and friends have been there, and I want to see what they're doing that I'm not."

He glanced at Margo and then back to the road. She smiled, "So this is really just a business date?"

He chuckled. "Well, I guess it's both. I wanted to spend time with you. And I wanted to get out of town so we could spend time talking to each other. But hey, I'm a business-man, so yeah, I'm gonna write it off because I want to make the Sandbar the best restaurant it can possibly be."

She turned in her seat and looked at him. He chanced a

glance one more time. Man, she had the most beautiful eyes.

"I think that's fair, but I also think you already have a pretty incredible place. People are happy there, Jace. What you've done is fantastic, and you are really good with people. When you told me the other night how much you enjoyed it, I started looking at it from that perspective, and you do look like you're happy there and enjoying it, and that's what makes customers want to come back. If you were stomping around and growly all the time, people would stop coming in. But you make them enjoy themselves because you're enjoying yourself. That's tremendous."

His heartbeat sped up. His cheeks even warmed. "Thank you. I appreciate you saying that." He navigated a corner. "How are you doing, Margo?"

She let out a breath. "You know, I know I'm gonna be alright. This was a betrayal I surely did not see coming. But to be honest with you, if Logan hadn't died, we probably wouldn't have been together much longer anyway. He had kind of started his life, I suppose, with Sierra, and I just kept working. He was gone. He was off having fishing trips, he said. I thought he had just, you know, found a lot of hobbies, and I poured myself into my work. I've now been realizing Carley's been helping me, and so have you. I wasn't really in a marriage for the last seven years. We were almost just business part- ners, sometimes sharing a house. The fact that the betrayals kept falling on me. Sierra. Changing his will. The stolen neck- lace. Each time something came to light, it made me realize even more that we didn't have a life together. I don't know how much longer he would have tolerated or put up with having two lives because he was actually living two lives. It was his own doing, of course, but I'm sure he would have tired of it sooner rather than later, and I would have been dealing with a lot of this stuff on my own anyway. The only difference I can see is that at least I may have had some closure by being able to tell him off or yell or scream." She shrugged, "Or, however that would have looked like coming to an end. But I'm gonna be fine. In so many ways, I kind of already am. Sure, it hurts. Sometimes I fall into thinking about things and wonder why. I think that's the biggest thing of all. I don't know why. Why would he change his will without just saying I want a divorce? And as he was dying, what did he think was going to come of this? That's the thing I don't know. I have never done anything to harm him. I don't know why he would want me to be hurt so badly. But it's over and done with now."

He felt bad listening to her story. A betrayal of an affair is one thing, the continuing betrayals were quite another. "I'm really sorry that you've had to go through this, Margo. Can I look at the bright side?"

She turned her head and her brows rose into her bangs. "Sure, what is the bright side?"

He grinned. "We wouldn't be on this date if he were still alive. Maybe."

She laughed. "You're right there. I'm not the cheating kind."

He reached over and picked up her hand and lay their hands together on the console of his pickup. They interlaced their fingers, and more than once, he looked down at their interlocking fingers. Their hands looked good together. His hands were tanned; hers were lighter. His fingers were bigger; hers were smaller. Her skin was soft, but his was not. The way her hand felt in his made his body warm all over. It was like her size was made just for him. And he liked holding her hand. He liked talking with her. He liked looking over and seeing her sitting in his truck. More than just the fact that she was incredibly beautiful. There was just something about her. Even with at all the trauma she'd gone through recently, in a short amount of time, she was calm. She was fighting a war within herself for all the things that had fallen on her, but outwardly she was calm, and she made him feel calmer.

He liked that.

He pulled into the parking lot and regretfully had to let go of her hand. He parked his truck and hopped out quickly. He strode around the front of the truck and opened her door. He held his hand out for her to use as she alighted from the truck. He didn't let go as they walked into the restaurant.

When they entered the restaurant, he couldn't help but turn to look at the decorating. He leaned down close to her ear, and in a conspiratorial whisper, he said, "So if you see something interesting you'd like to point out, I'd love your thoughts. Let's do this together."

She laughed. "Okay, well, I can look at it as a real estate agent would look at them or a customer. What I like and don't like. But I'll be honest with you, Jace, I like your motif better. Surfboards, flip-flops, and umbrellas are so much more appealing than fish. There are pictures of crabs, lobsters, and turtles, and none of that is appealing to me as a customer. Kind of makes me think something might stink somewhere along the way. Fishy, you know? What you have going on at the Sandbar speaks of fresh air, sunshine, and happiness and being out in the water, and I think it's perfect."

He tried not to puff his chest out at her praise, but he felt taller than an old oak right now. They approached the hostess counter. "Two, please."

The hostess, who seemed about eighteen, with a blonde ponytail, nodded. "Yeah, come right this way."

He continued to hold Margo's hand as they followed her to the table. The hostess laid two menus on a table. "Here you go. Your server will be here shortly."

He let go of Margo's hand but held her chair out. He strode around the table and sat across from her. He looked into her eyes and smiled. "So you know, as soon as we close on Friday, I'm bulldozing the thrift shop and expanding the Sandbar. It's going to look cleaner and fresher, but I think you're right with the surfboards, umbrellas, and flip-flops. And I'll put some sunglasses or things that speak to being outside in the warm fresh air and having fun relaxing and enjoying yourself."

She smiled at him, and his heartbeat quickened. "Perfect. I think it's perfect."

He grinned. "Glad to hear it. I think we've got a winning plan. Now we just have to tick the days away till Friday, and then again till Monday."

"Why Monday?"

"Oh, I managed to get on the agenda for the town council meeting on Monday to ask about expanding. Quinn, who happens to be pretty damn good at drawing buildings, even though he claims he's not, drew me a picture of what I'd like the Sandbar to look like after renovation, and he added a second story and said, 'Imagine the view.' Now, I can't imagine it without the second story."

"Oh," she gasped and clapped her hands quietly. "Oh my god, that would be fantastic. Of course, you would have a patio all the way across the front of the bar on the beach side so that customers could sit outside and eat."

He nodded. "Of course. Complete with ceiling fans overhead to circulate the air, and Hanna brought up little misters."

"Oh, that would be fantastic. Yes, on days like this last week, we've had in the high nineties, that would be so refreshing. I'm excited for you, Jace."

He chuckled. "I'm pretty excited myself. I never dreamed that I would be able to grow the bar to those proportions.

He reached across the table and took her hands. "I have you to thank, partially anyway. You helped me get the thrift shop."

She chuckled. "Well at the time I took the offer to Lorraine, I wasn't too happy with you, but I'm glad it worked out."

He squeezed her hands. "I'm glad it worked out too."

They enjoyed a nice meal. They chatted about the restaurant and her plans for the real estate company. She wanted to make it bigger. He could see her doing it, she was determined, and she was good at what she did. She'd grow it for sure. He hoped he would be around with her to see it happen.

As he drove her home, he knew he wanted to see her again, and often, but he wanted to do this right. He parked in the driveway and helped her out of the truck. He walked her to the house, holding her hand. At the front door, she turned to him and grinned. "Is this where I ask you in for a drink?"

He tossed his head back and laughed. "I'll tell you what, I know you have Carley inside, and I don't want to disturb her. I think what I want to do is this." He leaned in and kissed her lips. It wasn't just a peck, his lips covered hers softly, his tongue sought entrance to her mouth, and she opened. Their tongues danced together. Their lips moved together. It was warm and soft and seductive. What he knew was he wanted more of this, but not tonight. They kissed while his body responded to her hands wrapping around his waist. Her hands splayed across his back, and he liked the way she felt against him. When their kiss ended, they were both a bit breathless. He looked into her eyes briefly and smiled. "I'd like to do this again."

She chuckled. "Me too."

He kissed her forehead, "Good night, Margo. How about tomorrow I make dinner for you at my place?"

Her eyes rounded and her lips, still wet from his kiss tilted into a beautiful smile. "I'd like that."

"I'll send you my address during the day tomorrow. Should we plan six again?"

"Six works."

He stepped back, winked at her, and turned toward his truck. Yeah, he was gonna woo her.

22

M argo's phone kept chiming. She had heard it for a while but couldn't wake up. She'd had too many sleepless nights, and it finally caught up with her last night. And for the first time in more than two weeks, she went to bed with her heart feeling like it was mending. She didn't have that heavy sense of dread when she lay down. What she had were visions of Jace Marriott in her head, smiling at her, holding her hand, kissing her. That was the best part.

Her phone chimed again, and she blinked several times, then rolled over to take her phone off the charging cradle. She looked at her phone and saw a text from a number she didn't know. Tapping the first one, she opened it up, and an instant fire began burning in her tummy.

"It's Sierra, I want to work at Price Realty. I don't know why you wouldn't want extra help. Logan wanted this for me. As a matter of fact, he told me just before he got sick that he was going to bring me into the real estate company. We were going to open a Miami office and work there together."

Margo huffed out a deep breath and laid back on a pillow. This woman! Did she wrong her in a different life or something?

Margo ran different options through her head, which was too early for anything before coffee. But, her non-coffee, sleepy brain came up with these options. She could respond, which she wanted to do, but what she wanted to say was probably not wise. Or she could just block her phone number. That was probably the best thing to do. She could always unblock her later if she needed to. Yes, that was probably the smartest thing. So that's what she did. She tapped Sierra's text, scrolled to the words, *block this caller*, and tapped. Then she rolled herself out of bed, used the bathroom, and stumbled down the hall to the kitchen. Carley wasn't awake yet, but the coffee had already brewed. Pouring herself a cup of coffee, she ran scenarios through her head. Sitting in the living room, in the far corner of the sofa, she curled her feet under her. She dropped her phone on the sofa and saw a text message that she'd missed last night. Taking a deep breath before looking at it, she saw Jace's name.

"I had a nice time tonight, thank you."

Oh, she missed it. That made her feel sad.
She tapped his text and responded right away,

"I had a nice time too. I'm sorry I just saw this. I fell asleep quickly last night."

Jace responded with a smiley face and then he replied,

"I thought I'd grill you the finest steak you've ever had tonight. Are you a meat eater?"

She laughed, then she replied,

"Of course I eat meat. Steak sounds fantastic."

He responded with a happy face back and she figured he was probably getting ready to go to work. So she scrolled through social media a little bit and then checked the news to see if there was anything pressing in the world today that she needed to be aware of. That heavy feeling settled in the pit of her stomach, so she decided to just enjoy her coffee without any of the noise.

Carley woke and stumbled down the hall.

Margo smiled. "Good morning."

"Good morning," Carley said. "Do you need more coffee?"

"Yes, if you wouldn't mind refilling, I would appreciate that."

Carley took her cup and slogged to the kitchen.

None of them had been morning people, her and her three sisters. They got that from their mom. She hadn't been a morning person either. She used to tell them when they were little, "Please just let me have one cup of coffee before we have to start talking about anything and making decisions."

At the time, Margo thought it was incredibly rude. Now she totally understood it.

Carley came back out, handed her a cup of coffee, and then sat in the opposite corner of the sofa and tucked her feet up under her just like Margo did.

She watched her sister and smiled.

Carley sipped her coffee, and Margo decided to honor their mother and her sister and not say anything until Carley was ready. She stared out at her flowers, which she could see from this corner of the sofa. It's why she always sat there. The birds flew around; bees were buzzing. It was peaceful right now.

"How was your date last night?" Carley finally asked.

"It was good. Really good."

"That's nice. Where'd you go?"

"We went to the Crab Shack in Spring Harbor."

"Oh, I've heard about that place. I think Grace mentioned something about it."

Margo smiled. "It was nice. For Jace, it was half date, half business."

"What does that mean?" Margo chuckled and told Carley about the decor and Jace's plans for the Sandbar.

"Oh well, you're the perfect person to help out with that. You're very good at decorating."

" Thank you, Carley. What did you do last night?"

"I read part of a book and then fell asleep. When I woke up, I tried to read some more but fell asleep again, so I just decided to go to bed. I guess all of us have been light on sleep the last few weeks."

"Yeah, how are you feeling about your breakup with Don and everything?"

"I'm actually fine. I was so tired of the fighting. So tired of the bickering. And he got to the point where everything I did, he found fault with. I got really tired of that. Actually, I was stressed by it. If I tried to cook, he would point out faults. If I cleaned something, he would point out how I didn't do it the way he thought it should be done. After a while, it got to the point where I was afraid to do anything because I felt like I was going to be criticized. And then I got criticized for not doing anything."

Margo shook her head. "I'm sorry Carley."

Carley shrugged. "It's okay. I mean it's not okay, but it's okay. I'm fine. I have felt so much better being here and out of that environment. I can't even explain to someone how just removing yourself from that is so stress-relieving and freeing. I thank you, Margo, for letting me stay here."

Margo reached forward and patted Carley's leg. "It's okay, honey, you're always welcome here. And I guess we needed each other, right?"

"Right. That's right. So now what's going on today?"

Margo took a breath, "Well I woke this morning to texts from Sierra telling me how she wanted to work at the real estate office and how Logan promised to open a Miami office and have her work there with him. So I blocked her."

Carley covered her mouth with her hand. Swallowed the coffee in her mouth and then looked at Margo. She laughed and then grinned. "Good for you. I'm glad you did that. That stupid bitch. Who does she think she is anyway?"

"Yeah, I don't know. Jace told me that he thinks she's a gold digger. I don't know what Logan did to make her think that he had enough money to be a sugar daddy. I suppose he gave her the necklace. And obviously, they flew places. They went here and there, but it's not like we're multi-million-aires. We have money. I have money, actually." She froze, her brows bunched together. "You know what? I have money. I need to clear this with Grant Parks, but it seems like Logan didn't give anything away to Sierra except 10% of the real estate company. Actually, 5%, but he didn't give her any money. It's all mine. Even the trust. I need to talk to Grant. I don't think we fully went through everything with the will when I was there." She stared at her sister. "Carley, I have money!"

Carley grinned at her sister. "I'm glad you do. You deserve it, Margo. You're the one who's been working hard for it."

Her heartbeat quickened. "Yeah, well, as soon as Grant's office opens this morning, I'll give him a call." She looked down at her watch. "And I have a date tonight."

Carley sipped at her coffee. The smile on her on her face turned up a notch. She turned her head and looked at her sister. "A date. Another one. That's three nights in a row you will have seen each other."

Margo shrugged. "Well, not really. I mean, we were at his place the other night, so that doesn't really count. We weren't on a date. Last night was a date. Tonight, he's making me steak at his place."

Carley's eyes rounded and her brows rose into her bangs. "Ooh at his place. Awesome!" She leaned forward and patted Margo's leg. " I'm so happy for you. Did you enjoy yourself with him?"

"I sure did. I did. It was nice. He held my hand. We talked. It was different than Logan. I like being near him. He's... I don't know what to say. I guess I feel safe with him. Like he's... he's got my back. He would never betray me. I don't believe he ever would. I don't know how you could know that about someone so quickly, but I just feel it. I never felt that with Logan as I look back on it. Never."

Carley nodded. "I think that's a sign. You know they always say trust your gut." Carley smiled. "Trust your gut, Margo. If you have a good gut feeling about him run with it. Good for you."

Margo nodded. She sipped at her coffee. It was good for her. She finished her coffee and stood. "Okay, I better get ready for work. I have arrangements to make with the title company today for Jace's closing on Friday. They should be ready to start wiring money now, so I'm gonna get that going, and then I don't know, I think we'll see if there are messages about any showings I have to do. The usual. What are you gonna do today, Carley?" She stopped and stared at her sister. "Do you have... are you working from home now? What's going on with you?"

Carley's lips turned down into a frown. "You know, I'm thinking about calling and quitting my job. I've been on vacation these last few weeks. I have so much time built up, but I don't really like it there, and I want to be here. And I don't know, I thought I would look for work here. There's probably not a lot, but I thought I would try to look for work here."

Margo shrugged. "Well, I think I might have an availability for an agent at the real estate office if you think you want to try your hand at real estate. I think you mentioned it a few years ago. If you like it, eventually, you will have to take the classes and get your license, but I'm happy to help you along the way."

"Really? Margo, that's fantastic. I never...I mean, don't pity me. Don't offer me a pity job. But if you think you'd really like to work with me, I'll work very hard for you. I'll do the best job I can do, and I know I'll have the best teacher."

Margo chuckled. "I know you'll work hard. I'm not worried about your work ethic at all and with your experience in marketing at large corporations, I think you'll be invaluable."

"Okay, what do you want me to do?" Carley's excitement began to rub off on her.

"Well, this morning, we'll go to the office and muck out Logan's office. You can have that. He only had seven things in the pipeline, and one closes next week so that's what I'll have you do. I'll have you call the buyer's agent on that closing and the title company. I'll walk you through that. What do you think?"

"That's fantastic. Thank you. Yes, thank you. Yes." Carley jumped up and hurried down the hall. Margo chuckled as she watched her older sister.

Of the four sisters, the order of their birth was Carley, Margo, Holly, and then Josseline. They were all two years apart as if they'd all been perfectly timed. Margo was now 43 years old. Carley was 45. She'd been married and divorced, and she'd been with Don for a long time. Long enough that they bought a house together. But thank goodness Carley didn't marry him. He was a turd. At least all the sisters thought so, though they didn't berate Carley for it. So now, she had a new chance at life, and Margo was excited to help her sister. Lord knows Carley had helped her so much over her life, but these last few weeks especially.

Margo showered and entered the kitchen to see Carley whipping up breakfast for them. "I'm making an omelet. Is an omelet good for you?"

Margo chuckled. "An omelet is perfect for me."

They ate breakfast together, drank another cup of coffee, and then went to the office together. The office was located on First Street, and she could pull into the driveway and park behind the building. It was just before nine. Her assistant, Addison, was already there.

"Good morning, Margo."

"Good morning. Addison, this is my sister Carley. Carley is going to be trying out the real estate business to see if it's something she's interested in. In the meantime, I'm going to have her in Logan's office. Can you please pull up for her the real estate deals that Logan had in the pipeline? I know there were seven of them but get the paperwork and the file names for her so she can keep those files and the others. We'll clean out Logan's office."

Addison smiled. "Well, it's nice to meet you, Carley." She reached her hand out, and they shook hands. "I'll get right on the files. Also, there are a couple of messages here. I took them off the voicemail. I don't quite understand them, but someone wants to work here. Sierra, something?"

Margo closed her eyes. When she opened them, she looked at Addison for a moment, who was watching her. She huffed out a breath. "I may as well tell you this. You'll likely hear it anyway. Sierra Stigler was Logan's mistress. They've been having an affair for seven years. Logan changed his will two years ago to give Sierra Stigler ten percent of this company. What I've managed to figure out, with the help of Grant Park, is that he is only allowed to give ten percent of his half of the company which is five percent of the entire company. And even that is suspect. As a matter of fact, I need to call Grant and find out what he managed to root out after looking through our incorporation papers."

Addison frowned. "I'm sorry, Margo. I had no idea Logan was involved with anyone else."

Margo shook her head. "You couldn't have known that anyway, and don't worry, I'm managing all of this...mess."

Addison nodded her head. Her voice was soft when she replied, "On that note, Grant Park left you a message to call him. It's also in these."

She handed over several pink slips of paper that she had pulled off the voicemail.

"Thank you. I'll get Carley situated in Logan's office and then if you could pull those files, I'll work with her after I call Grant. In the meantime, Sierra Stigler is not working here. She has nothing to say about anything that goes on in this company, and if she comes in here, tell her to leave. If she won't leave just call the police. We don't want her here and we're not going to deal with her drama and pettiness. I'm just not gonna do it."

Addison nodded. "Okay, thank you."

Margo looked at Carley and nodded toward the set of doors. Logan and Margo had offices side by side. Their company was small. There were only two other rooms across the hall from their two offices, one was their file room. All their real estate dealings were filed by the last name of the seller and placed on shelves in alphabetical order. They kept them for seven years, and at the end of the seventh year, Addison would clean out those seven-year files and make sure they were scanned into their system, and then she destroyed the documents. She didn't have anything original here anyway other than the offers, and at that point, after they had been closed for seven years, there was no need to keep that either.

The second room was their conference room. It wasn't large, but it served as a clean place to meet with prospective buyers and sellers. It was comfortable and sensibly deco-rated with pictures of Blossom Springs and the sunsets.

She opened Logan's door, which she hadn't opened since he'd died. She was pleased to see that it was in fairly good order. Addison called out, "I straightened up a week ago. I didn't know what to do, and I was feeling kind of sad, so any files that were closed for a while that he had stacked on the corner of the desk, I just filed them away. I hope that's okay, I can get you a list of them."

Margo shook her head and smiled at her loyal assistant. "It's not necessary. Thank you for taking the initiative, Addison."

Carley stepped in and looked around. "Wow this is...this is amazing, Margo. Thank you so much. I'm so excited to start working with you. And to have my own office, which is very nice, I'm feeling a bit overwhelmed and so frigging excited. I can't wait to tell Holly and Josseline."

Margo chuckled. "I'm glad to hear that. So why don't you get yourself situated? If you need to rearrange the drawers and put things where you want them, feel free to do so. In the meantime, I'll have Addison set you up with a username and password so you can log into our system, and then we will show you how to use it. While you're doing that, I'm going to go call Grant. I'm right next door if you need anything, and Addison knows everything you need to know, so you should feel free to ask her."

"Thank you, Margo." Carley hugged her, and Margo's heart felt so good to help her sister. Plus, she loved Carley, and it was wonderful having someone you love working with you.

She moved down the hall to Addison's desk. "Can you help her get set up and issue her a username and password for the software? Then, if you don't mind, can you walk her through the software?"

Addison smiled brightly. It had likely been rather quiet in the office recently, and she was likely happy to have something to do. "Sure, thank you so much I'm happy to do that."

Margo smiled and nodded. "Thank you so much for everything, Addison."

She turned and strode into her office. Sitting in her desk

chair she took a deep breath before picking up her desk phone.

As Grant answered she grinned. "Good morning."

"Good morning, how are you, Margo?"

"I'm managing. How are you?"

"I'm good. I just wanted to give you the news. Logan did not have proper authority to give away any shares in your company. It was not done appropriately. We have your record book here as you know, and we drafted your annual minutes. There's nothing in the minutes that states that anything was brought up for a vote and voted on. Which is the procedure. I will be calling Sierra Stigler's attorney today and letting him know that she doesn't have any shares in the company and is not entitled to any."

Margo took a deep breath. It felt like a weight had been lifted, even though she knew this from her perspective. To have Grant confirm, made her feel more comfortable. "I can't even tell you how happy I am to hear that. Not even for the money but just to know that Logan's last little knife in my back didn't amount to anything. I also got a text from Sierra this morning saying she wanted to work here, and Logan had promised her a Miami location of Price Realty."

Grant huffed out a breath. "Well, good luck to her. I'll tell you that she can't incorporate as Price Realty Inc. in Miami if she wants to because you already have that incorporation in the state of Florida. So she'll have to come up with another name if she wants to start her own company."

Margo smiled. She leaned back in her chair and let her back rest. "I wanted to talk to you about one other thing. Money. We didn't get to that in your office the other day when you talked about Logan's will. We were both so stunned by what he had done that we didn't talk about money. So, any money that came through the real estate company is mine, as you just confirmed, but we had a trust set up with money in it, and I believe he was not able to transfer anything out of the trust. I'm the trustee and I didn't transfer anything out. Am I clear on that? Any money we have in the trust is all mine now?"

Grant responded quickly, "You're right on that. All the money is yours. Do you know how much there is in there?"

Margo shook the mouse on her computer and called up their financial planning website. "Let me look here, hang on." She logged in and waited a moment while it loaded. She read the columns and balances for the various stocks their portfolio was invested in. She scrolled down to the bottom and saw the final total. "It looks like we have close to ten million dollars in this account."

Her heart hammered in her chest. She had no idea it had grown to that amount.

Grant laughed. It was unexpected, but it made her so happy. "Good for you, Margo. Good for you. And that is all yours."

She chuckled right along with him. Her heart felt happy once again, and it had nothing to do with the money, it had to do with the fact she was winning.

23

Jace was in a great mood. It had been a great night. Although he ended it differently than he would have liked to, he really meant it, he was gonna woo her. She'd been through a tough time recently. Betrayal was a hard thing to get over, and while he had told her, and he believed she believed him, he was nothing like Logan. There would always be those niggly doubts until they got to know each other a little bit better, and he wanted to get to know her better.

Hanna came in and brought fresh cinnamon rolls for everyone. That always made his staff happy. The mood in the kitchen was lively today. It usually was but now they were all on a sugar high. The closing on the thrift shop was in two days. There was excitement within the company about the expansion. Everyone felt like this place had a great future.

And it did. He was happy that he'd made the decision when he first bought this place to hire only veterans. These folks served their country, and a lot of them needed the help. They needed to feel needed. They needed the reprieve from feeling like they didn't exactly belong. That was the hard part about getting out of the military. You felt like you didn't belong anywhere. Veterans who saw battle saw things many could not comprehend. It changed a person. It altered your brain. As a result, you didn't feel like a regular person anymore. But you were. It was just that others didn't understand you and what you'd been through. Here, they all understood each other.

Everywhere he went, people would ask him where he served or if he served, and when he said that he did, they would say, 'Oh yeah, I was gonna go in the service too, but I decided...whatever.' He was so sick of hearing people say how they were gonna do that too, but they didn't for whatever reason. If you didn't, you didn't. Don't tell a veteran that you thought about it. It's like they were just trying to ride on their coattails or something. It was fucking annoying. It was hard enough dealing with everyday life without all that bullshit.

So, when he bought this place, he made the decision to hire only veterans. That was the rule he told everyone when he hired them. You don't tell anybody, 'Oh yeah, I was gonna go in that branch of the service, but the food sucks.' or 'I was gonna go in that branch of service because of whatever. You didn't.' You didn't go to that branch of service.

You went in the branch of service you were with. Be happy about that. Be proud of it. Proud of your service. Proud of your fellow co-workers because they had done it too. That was it. It made for a better environment here.

He finished setting up the tables outside. Theresa was out raking the sand. Mason had the bar all set up and ready to go for lunch, and he had a moment. He pulled his phone out and texted Margo his address. Then he called her.

"Well, hello there," she said.

"Hi, I just texted you my address."

"Oh," she said "I didn't see. Hang on I'm gonna look."

When she responded, she sounded surprised. "Isn't that the Governor's Mansion?"

He chuckled. "That it is."

"Do you own it?"

"I do."

"When did you buy it?"

He chuckled. "Why all the questions?"

"Well, I didn't even know it had been for sale. That place has been sitting there empty as long as I can remember."

"It was, but it just worked out that I had a friend who had some knowledge of the former family and contacted them privately. They were all excited for a private sale, so we quietly made the deal."

"Well, I'll be," she said softly. "Aren't you the sly one? And I missed out on a commission."

He laughed. "I'm sorry about the commission, but I was glad to get the deal done."

"Was it in good shape?"

"Yeah, it was all right. I mean, some things had fallen into disrepair from sitting, and you know the humidity here and such. Luckily, they had kept the heat and air conditioning on. Even though they had the air turned up to eighty-five, it did keep the place from getting moldy. But I've had it completely remodeled since then, thanks to my friend Quinn, and now it's just my home sweet home."

Margo laughed. The sound of her laugh was melodic and sexy. The little deep undertone she had kind of did something to him. The hair on his arms stood up.

"Okay, so you'll be over at six?"

"Yes, I'll be over at six. Can I bring something?"

"Nope, I've got this covered. Just bring yourself. And a smile."

She laughed again and he closed his eyes to listen to the sound.

"All right, I'll see you then."

She ended the call, and he whistled as he took the empty dishwasher racks and glasses back to the kitchen. As he came back out, he was still whistling and had a little skip in his step until he saw Sierra walking into the bar.

"Mother of ass," he muttered.

He quickly spun around and stepped back into the kitchen. "Jose, are you ready to wait tables?"

"I am."

"Can you please take care of the redhead? She just walked in."

"Sure thing."

Maybe she'd appreciate a male server instead of a female, not that he wanted Jose to have to deal with bullshit. He would handle that if it came to that. But he knew he didn't want to have anything to do with her. Jose exited the kitchen and Jace went outside and began setting up the new Tiki bar that he had just had Quinn's crew build. It wasn't finished quite yet, but it was certainly operational enough that they could have basic drinks, beer in the coolers, and their Sandbar Punch, so the servers didn't have to go all the way inside when refilling drinks. It would make things easier for them. And the best part, boaters and swimmers who were hanging out on the sandbar could walk up and not have to go inside to get drinks. Win-win. He was all about winning.

24

Margo peeked in on Carley to see how she was settling in and getting familiar with the software and files. "How are you doing?"

Carley looked up from the computer screen and grinned. "I'm doing good, I think. I managed to log in. I've checked the seven properties that Logan has under contract, and I even managed to click into them to see what the status was on each one."

Margo laughed. "I knew you'd be good at this. You're smart with computers and with your administrative skills, this is a piece of cake. As soon as we have the opportunity, I'll get you through some of the actual *realtor-type* business."

"That sounds good. Thanks, Margo."

Margo's cell phone rang. Quinn Kurtz was on the screen. "Hey, Quinn how are you doing?"

He chuckled. "I'm doing well. How are you, Margo?"

"I'm doing well. What can I help you with?"

"Well as it turns out, the first three units in my barracks project are ready to be sold. I was hoping that you would like to be the listing agent on those."

"Oh absolutely. I just hired my sister, Carley, as a realtor. She doesn't have her license yet, but she's learning, and I'll bring her over to take a look at them as well. It can be one of her first big projects. We'll work on them together."

Quinn chuckled. "Well, that's two for the price of one. I can't beat that right?"

"That's right," Margo chuckled. "What's a good time for us to come over and take a look at what you have?"

"I'm here now. I'll be here for another two hours. We're shoring up some work in the upstairs. Those aren't quite ready yet, but I'm working with Jared on them now, and I can give you a better update on timing for those when you get here."

"Great!" Margo glanced at Carley and held her hand up.

Carley nodded.

"We'll leave here now and be there shortly."

"Great, Margo, thanks. I'll see you in a little bit." Quinn ended the call and Margo looked across the office at her sister. "Did you hear any of that or most of that?"

"I heard some of it. I think I heard Quinn's voice and he's got something for sale."

"Yes, the first three condos in his barracks project are ready, and we are the listing agent on that."

"Oh, how exciting!" Carley's smile lit up the room.

"So, here's what I want you to do. Go to the file room. Did Addison show you all of that?"

"Yes, she did."

"Okay, awesome. Go to the file room and bring up five Listing Contracts, a Property Condition Report, the Well Water Report, and the Sewage Report. Then let me know when you're ready. I'm going to use the restroom."

"Sounds good."

Carley hustled out of the office and across the hall to the file room. Margo grinned. She hadn't seen Carley this excited in quite a while, and then she felt bad for not paying attention to her sister's sadness. She had just stuck her head into work, so she didn't realize how unhappy anybody was, including herself.

She used the restroom, washed her hands, and came out to find Carley waiting. "I'm so excited for this. I brought extra of everything in case I make a mistake."

Margo laughed. "Well, actually, what we're going to do is go through the listing. You will hand write information in. We'll then bring it back to the office and type it up, so everything is neat and clean. I didn't know if you were quite ready for that in front of a customer, even one who is a friend, so I thought we'd come back and do it ourselves. Then, we can send it to him as an e-document to sign. He's done this before and is perfectly comfortable with it, so this is good practice for you."

"Excellent! I'm so excited. I can't believe my first day we're able to get a listing."

Margo smiled at her sister's excitement. "You're good luck, Carley."

Her sister hugged her quickly and kissed her cheek. "You're good luck, Margo."

Oh, her heart swelled. She grabbed her purse from her desk and strode toward the back door. As she neared Addison's desk, she said, "We'll be gone for a little while. I don't know if you heard all this hustle and bustle."

Addison grinned broadly. "I did. That's good news."

"It is. So we'll be back around lunchtime. Will you be here?"

"Actually, I have lunch plans with my mom. Is that okay?"

"Perfectly okay, Addison. I just thought we would treat you to lunch. How about tomorrow?"

"Tomorrow is good."

"We'll have lunch; just the three of us, just to get to know each other a little better. How about that?"

"Thanks, Margo. That sounds great."

Margo grinned and turned toward the door. Carley was right next to her.

As she backed out of her parking space, Carley asked, "Can you tell me a little bit about where everything is in town? Since I'm not from here, I probably should know a little bit more."

Margo glanced at her sister and nodded. "I forgot about that. Okay sure. Margo's office was located on First Street. She pulled out of the driveway and turned left on First Street. Then turned left on Main Street. "So to the left here is the grocery store. I think you're familiar with that."

Carley laughed. "I am. I've been there a couple of times."

"Good. And on the right here is the ice cream shop. Next to the ice cream shop is the insurance office. Next to that the laundromat. And then next to that is the nail salon. That's where I always go."

"Oh, I'm gonna have to try them. Your nails always look awesome."

Margo grinned. She was beginning to feel pretty darned special, and it had been a long time since that feeling had been in her head.

"Next to the grocery store on the left is the barber shop and then Williams' Hardware."

She continued down Main Street, "And right at the end of Main Street, is the old barracks. So we drive straight into the barracks. I'm going to have to ask him if he's changing the name. He was going to get rid of the barracks name, but I'm not sure if he did."

They pulled into the parking lot next to Quinn's truck. Just as she parked, Quinn stepped out of the main door. He waited for them to each get out of the vehicle and sauntered towards them.

"Hello there, ladies."

Margo grinned. "Hi, Quinn."

Carley was more enthusiastic. She couldn't stop smiling. "Hi, Quinn. I'm really excited for this opportunity."

He chuckled. "I am too. Well, come right in. Let me show you what we have here."

They stepped into the front room of the first building. It was open and bright. There was a pool table in the middle of the room. The back wall was a line of cabinets and a countertop. To the right of that was a refrigerator, and there was a sink next to the refrigerator. A dishwasher was below the counter next to the sink. "So this is the common area." Quinn started his tour. "Any condo owner will have access to this area. Once we have the condos full enough, the owners will then vote on an association board, and the association will be responsible for keeping track of this. Eventually, you won't walk right into this area because if somebody wanted to rent it out for a private party, that wouldn't be very private. So there will be glass walls here that create a little bit of a hallway, but it'll be open and bright."

Margo nodded. "You've done a nice job here, Quinn."

"Thank you. We're very happy with how it's turning out. It's been a lot of work but it's looking good."

"I'll say."

Quinn moved toward the hallway, Margo and Carley were right behind him. To the right of the hallway was the first unit. "There will be four units down here on the first floor and six units upstairs. That's because the upstairs doesn't have a common area. Down here are all one-bedroom units. Upstairs are all two-bedroom units. Those will be ready in about two months. Right now, the three units down here are finished, and the far one at the end should be ready shortly. I'll say a few weeks."

Carley looked around and smiled. "It looks really nice here."

Quinn nodded. "Thank you." They meandered through the condo. He showed them the kitchen, the amenities, the showers, the bathroom, and the bedroom and then walked them down to the next one. He continued with his tour. "Each of these units is identical, and, of course, when someone buys, they're welcome to change it up however they want. But for selling purposes, all the walls will be white. All the kitchens will have beige and copper granite counters and white cabinetry. From there, it's up to the individual buyers what they want."

Margo nodded. "That's great, Quinn. It looks very nice. Do you think there'd be the opportunity to change some of the units up for a little variety when showing them?"

Quinn looked at her and cocked his head to the side. "I hadn't thought of that."

Margo nodded. "Well, if you wanted to have a couple of the units with dark cabinets and maybe a lighter granite, it doesn't have to be anything big, just a little variation in how the kitchen looks mostly. Kitchens and baths are so important."

"Okay, well, I think that shouldn't be a problem. Let me talk to the architect about that, and we'll get that scheduled for the upstairs units since these downstairs ones are already finished. And since I have two more buildings to remodel, it shouldn't be a problem at all making changes over there."

"Perfect."

They finished their tour and then sat down in the common room at the small folding table. The regular furniture had not been delivered yet.

Margo let Carley write out the Listing Contract. She did a good job asking all the questions of Quinn, who was very patient with her. Carley wrote it up.

Margo smiled at her when she was finished. Carley glanced at Quinn. "We're going to take this back and type it all up, then I'll email it to you to e-sign it."

He chuckled. "That sounds good. I'll watch for it."

Margo stood and hugged Quinn. "Thank you, Quinn. May I ask what you've decided to call these condo units and this association?"

He chuckled, "Well, we've just decided to keep it The Barracks. I know that sounds different and maybe uninviting, but I've asked the staff over at the Sandbar and my own employees, who are all veterans, and they all like the idea of just keeping it The Barracks. It speaks to former service members. So that's what we're gonna do."

"Fair enough. I think that sounds great. That also helps when looking for buyers, which shouldn't be that hard."

They exited the building, and on their way back to the real estate office, Margo said, "Are you up for lunch?"

Carley chuckled. "Oh my gosh, yes! I would absolutely love that. Actually, I'd like to buy."

Margo turned down Main Street and turned left on Sunset Beach Road. She parked her SUV and excitement ran through her at seeing Jace.

25

Jace glanced toward the front of the bar as he waited for Mason to mix his drinks. Margo and Carly entered the Sandbar and spoke to the hostess. She nodded her head and led them to a table in the corner. His smile was instantaneous. His heart beat a little faster, and he couldn't help but admire how beautiful she looked again today. It seemed to be the norm for her. No matter what she wore, she always looked elegant, refined, and incredibly sexy. Her eyes met his, and she waved. He strode toward her table, excited to chat with her. "Hello, ladies, what can I get you started with?"

Margo chuckled. "I'll take a raspberry iced tea."

Carley smiled. "Same. Please."

"Coming right up." He hustled to the bar and hung their drink order on the order board for Mason, picked up the tray of drinks waiting for him to deliver to their thirsty customers, and hurried outside to deliver them. As soon as he re-entered the restaurant, he scrambled to the bar, picked up Margo and Carley's teas, and delivered them to their table.

"Here you go, ladies. Raspberry iced tea."

They smiled at him, and he found it difficult to look away from Margo's smile. Laughter from another table brought him around to the task at hand - lunch.

"We have smoked salmon salad on a bed of spinach for our lunch special today."

Carley responded immediately. "I'll take that, please."

He wrote her order down on his order slip. "We have Asian ginger or balsamic dressing."

"Oh, I'll take the Asian ginger please."

He grinned, that was his favorite too. He turned his head to Margo and noticed her watching him. His heart skipped a beat. There was something about her.

She smiled sweetly "I'll have the same, please."

"You got it." He wrote her order down and noticed her shiver. "Are you cold?"

"I think the air conditioning is blowing right on me here. Maybe we should go outside and eat."

Jace leaned in. "Just so you know, Sierra's out there, so maybe you would want to stay inside?"

Margo nodded and took a deep breath. "Thank you for the heads up and absolutely we will stay inside. It feels good being cooled down."

He grinned and received a gorgeous smile in response.

Margo asked. "How did we get so lucky to have the owner also be our server?"

Jace grinned, he turned to see Carley sit back and cross her arms watching her sister play.

"I've been told I'm a flirt and then two beautiful women walked in while I happened to be at the bar, and what can I say? I jumped at the chance."

Margo grinned and he leaned down. "Is that derogatory?"

She turned her head and looked up at him. They stared into each other's eyes for a few moments, and then she burst out laughing. "No, it's not derogatory. I'm sorry I told you that."

He nodded. "All right just checking. I'll put your orders in."

He kept himself busy running orders and delivering drinks. When Margo's order came up, he hurried to pick them up and deliver them. Setting their salads in front of them, he set the dressings on the side. "Anything else I can get for you?"

He stared into Margo's eyes for a moment and the sexy look she gave him sizzled right through him. Carley chuckled and Jace thought, it boded well for this evening.

"No, thank you."

"Well, you two ladies are easy." He quipped.

Margo gave him a side eye, a half-smile on her face. "One thing I am not Jace, is easy."

He nodded. "Noted. I'll be back to check on you shortly."

He practically whistled and skipped back to the kitchen. He was beginning to see playful Margo, and he liked her a lot. He checked for his orders. Nothing was up yet, so he did a run-through of his tables for drinks. He did the same outside. As he made his way back to the restaurant, he noted that the workers were back to finish up the tiki bar. Hopefully, it wouldn't disrupt the lunch too much, but he wasn't going to tell them to go away. It was hard to get Quinn's crews back. They were busy as hell this time of year.

Carley strode past him to use the restroom, and he glanced to see Margo chatting with the woman at the table next to her. He grinned. He'd let her chat. He strode into the kitchen to check on things. All seemed in order. As he stepped back out to the restaurant, he noticed Carley moving toward her table and Sierra moving quickly toward her. Alarm bells went off at the look on Sierra's face, but before he could move, Sierra rammed into Carley and spilled an entire drink on her.

Carley looked down at her clothing, then up to stare at Sierra. He intervened quickly, as did Theresa, his server.

He nodded to Theresa, who put an arm around Carley. "Let me help you with this. I have towels in the office." She moved Carley to the back room and the office. He glared at Sierra. "That was uncalled for."

"It was an accident."

"It wasn't. I saw the whole thing. I'd like you to leave now."

"I was just coming to see if you'd like to have dinner tonight."

"No." He swallowed. "Leave now."

She tossed her red hair over her shoulder and glared at him. She inhaled deeply, then strode to the front door without looking back. If she had, she'd have seen him glaring at her and Margo doing the same thing.

Carley came back to the table in a few minutes and sat down.

He strode by to check on them. Just as he arrived, a loud bang, like the sound of lumber being dropped outside reverberated through the bar, and then Carley sat up staring at the bar. Jace slowly turned and saw Mason in a panic attack.

Jace hustled over to Mason. "Are you okay, bud? Do you need to sit down?"

He pulled a chair to the bar and helped Mason into the chair. It was as if he couldn't really see. Mason shook, and Jace kept his body in front of Mason to shield him from the people in the restaurant. The kitchen door opened, and Jose came out with some plates of food. Jace nodded at him, and Jose delivered his food quickly, then rushed back.

Jace whispered, "Get me some water for Mason."

"Will do." Jose hurried behind the bar and pulled a bottle of water from the cooler. Jace knelt next to Mason with his arm around his shoulders adding pressure. Boy, he wished Grace's support dog, Chiefy, was here right now. She was really good at this. And that's when he wondered if he should get a service dog for the restaurant. It was unusual with food prep. She probably couldn't ever be in the kitchen, but he'd check and see if a service animal could be in the bar or behind the bar. After a few moments, Mason's shaking subsided. Jace rubbed his back and handed him the bottle of water. "Take a couple of sips, Mason."

He did as he was asked, then shook his head. "I'm so fucking embarrassed."

"Don't be embarrassed. This is nothing to be embarrassed about."

"But everyone knows."

"It doesn't matter what everyone knows. And for the record, what everyone knows is that I hire only veterans here, so they know that you've served. And if they saw this panic attack, they know that you have PTSD. There is no shame in that, Mason. None at all. I have it. Sid has it. Quinn has it. Marco has it. Theresa has it. We all have it."

Mason shook his head. "I could have broken something. I could have dropped something. Something bad could have happened."

Jace nodded. "Shoulda, coulda, woulda. Something could happen to all of us today, Mason. I could walk out of here and get hit by a car. We can't live in fear of that." Jace stood and patted Mason on the shoulders. "Now, do you need to go home? Do you need to lay down? Do you want to just take a break? Tell me what you need right now, and I will help you."

Mason swallowed. He took a couple of deep breaths. He looked up at Jose who nodded. "It's all good bud. It's all good. We're all here for you."

Mason nodded. "I think if I can just take about a five-minute break, I'll be fine. I just want to go back and maybe eat a little something and just kind of shake this off."

Jace nodded. "Okay go do that. We're fine. Jose and I will watch the bar and take over. Do what you need to do."

Mason took a deep breath and slowly stood. He waited for his legs to steady under him, then he strolled to the kitchen. Jace checked orders at the bar.

Jose said, "Everything is calming down outside. I can handle the bar if you have things to do, Jace."

Jace grinned. "We'll take turns back here. Check our tables. Make sure everybody has drinks and then we'll switch. Sound good?"

"Sounds good. We've got this."

Jace chuckled. "I'll run by my tables quickly."

He swung through the restaurant checking tables. He stopped at Margo and Carley's table last. "You ladies need anything? Is everything okay?"

Margo reached over and put her hand over his. "That was beautiful."

He swallowed the knot that grew in his throat. "I only hire veterans Margo, and we all have issues with PTSD or other things. Sometimes it happens and I'm here to help. Always."

He saw tears glisten in her eyes. She pinched her lips together and sniffed slightly. "Well, again, that was beautiful."

Tears welled up in his eyes and emotion clogged his throat. He tried swallowing a couple of times. He turned his hand over and squeezed hers. He managed to get out. "I gotta go help at the bar. See you at six."

26

Margo drove up the driveway to Jace's home. She practically laughed when she saw the Governor's Mansion. And didn't it look beautiful? She hadn't been back here in ages. There was no need, and no one had even inquired about buying it.

Color her surprised when Jace told her he lived here. He owned it. So much for her top realtor status in Florida.

Before she could knock on the door it opened.

He smiled at her. "Welcome to Casa Marriott."

He bowed and ushered her in with his hand. She laughed. Stepped through the threshold and into the foyer.

He closed the door and the second he did she turned and wrapped her arms around his neck and kissed him passionately. Their lips blended together beautifully. His were soft and wet. And they molded perfectly to hers. She couldn't get the kiss from last night out of her head.

She couldn't remember the last time anybody had ever kissed her like that. Certainly not in years. And she didn't remember it feeling quite like this.

His hands wrapped around her body. They were strong

and firm, pulling her snugly to his body. A little moan escaped her throat, just feeling him pressed firmly against her.

It was so fucking exciting.

They kissed until they were breathless. And then he kissed down her cheek, her jaw, and her neck. She wore a spaghetti-strap white blouse. It was gauzy and fun. And his lips were able to kiss her shoulders. And then he kissed across her collarbone.

She dug her fingers into his hair and guided his head toward her breasts. He eagerly enjoyed the invitation. His firm fingers lifted her shirt, revealing a strapless bra.

He kissed over first one mound and then the other. Teasing her skin right where the bra started and her skin ended. His fingers slid around her ribs to her back.

He tucked a finger under her bra strap and pinched it with his thumb and the bra released. He tugged it from the front and let it fall to the floor and his mouth quickly sought her breasts.

He sucked one nipple in, and the lightning bolt that shot through her body and right to her core was hot, fast, and surprising.

She groaned again.

He stood and lifted her high on his waist. Her legs wrapped around him, and his mouth found her breasts once more.

His hands each cupped an ass cheek and squeezed firmly as his mouth suckled on her breasts. One, then the next, then back to the first one. Back and forth.

Her excitement reached a fever pitch. Her skin grew warm, and her heart beat so fast she felt dizzy. She couldn't stand it. She wanted Jace Marriott. She wanted him badly.

He elicited so many emotions in her right now.

He pulled back and stared up at her.

She stared down into his gorgeous brown eyes for a long time. She licked her lips and his eyes dipped to her tongue and then back up to her eyes.

"I want you, Jace."

"Thank fucking goodness." He stared a bit longer and when he responded, his voice was husky. "I want you too, Margo."

He carried her to the grand staircase. They circled the room as they ascended each step. It was almost ridiculous how excited she felt about all of this. Her passions had lay dormant for years. So long, in fact, she'd nearly forgotten how it felt to be desired and to desire.

As he carried her, which seemed effortless, he kissed her jaw, nipped at her shoulder, or kissed behind her ear. Oh, that kiss caused so many things to happen to her body. As soon as he reached the bedroom door, he stepped inside.

He hurried over to the bed and gently lay her on top. In a fluid motion, he reached down and pulled her denim skirt over her hips and down her legs. He repeated the same with her panties. The cool air swirled around her bare skin, and the look in his eyes made goosebumps form on her skin.

She still had her gauzy shirt on, but it was lifted high over her breasts. She lay there exposed to him. He took a deep breath and began removing his clothing. She shimmied out of her top, then watched as his beautiful body was exposed to her, one gorgeous piece at a time. His chest was toned for a fifty-something-year-old man. His arms, which she had enjoyed recently as he carried her, bulged with muscle.

Her eyes feasted on his body then slid up to see him watching her. Goosebumps formed again and moisture gathered between her legs. He slowly unzipped his cargo shorts and let them fall to the floor. She enjoyed watching his body appear before her slowly and followed his form down to toned thighs and an impressive erection.

My God, how long had it been? She was trying to remember when the last time she had sex with Logan was. It had been a long fucking time.

Years.

It was probably years.

How had she not known that?

Or asked him about it? Or wondered about it?

Jace leaned over her slowly. He was taking his time and she wanted him to hurry. She didn't want to wait anymore. His eyes stared into hers and it was as if she were locked into place and couldn't move. His eyes were beautiful. By themselves they were beautiful. Thick spikey lashes framed the deep brown orbs. His tanned skin and graying hair complimented each other impressively. She wondered why he wasn't taken. What was wrong with the women in this town? He leaned further toward her. They were inches apart.

"Do I need a condom, Margo?"

Oh, a condom. She hadn't even thought of a condom. Her eyes rounded.

She opened her mouth to take a breath, but she didn't know what to say. He grinned and winked.

He pulled back, opened the bedside table, and rummaged around a little bit.

He found a condom and she refused to think about him keeping them in that nightstand, in this room.

He ripped it open. Quickly rolled it on. And then he was back over her once more. His movements were fluid and sure and it excited the shit out of her.

"Are you sure?"

Finally, a question she could answer. "Yes."

"Me too."

He positioned his cock at her entrance and slowly slid inside of her. It was perfection. He never looked away. She didn't either. She wanted to watch him as he made love to her. It was electric.

Her body was so on fire. Her breathing came in bursts and every time he pushed himself into her body, she wanted to close her eyes and commit the feeling to memory. He filled her so completely. So...perfectly.

She continued to stare as her hands roamed his body. His muscles flexed and moved as he entered her again and again. It was unfreaking believable. He took his time. What she'd wanted quickly before, she now wanted to last. Every time he pushed into her, she wanted it to continue. He didn't disappoint. He began pushing into her and swirling slightly, hitting her clit perfectly. Her skin heated further, and that tingling feeling became more urgent, and he found that perfect spot each. And. Every. Time.

"You are so fucking beautiful," he growled.

Words didn't come to her. The feel of him entering her again and again consumed her brain.

She lifted her legs and wrapped them around his waist, and he groaned. She sighed.

She was unable to look away from him; she didn't want to either.

Her hands slid up his body until she reached his head. Framing his face with her hands, her thumbs smoothed over his cheeks.

"You are unbelievable," she whispered.

He grinned slightly and shook his head. "I beg to differ. You are unbelievable," he huffed out.

His hips moved faster, the urgency growing for release.

He continued adding pressure in the perfect spot every time he entered her.

She was so fucking close. Her breathing stuttered from her lungs, and her vision dimmed as the pressure between her legs grew.

She gasped as that hot pressure pushed her over the edge of desire. "Jace!" she whispered.

"Beautiful," he rasped.

He pulled out and entered her twice more, then closed his eyes as he let go.

Un-freaking-real.

27

Jace whistled as he made dinner for Margo. Making love to her was incredible. Their bodies fit together like two puzzle pieces. He tossed a salad, strode to the back door, started the grill, and poked holes in the potatoes.

The shower upstairs shut off and he grinned. He'd never brought a woman back to this place before. He tried so hard to keep it quiet that he even lived here. And since he'd been in town, which was two and a half years now, he'd just focused on business. He'd had his house remodeled, which required enough attention. Then there were things at the bar that needed repair. There was always so much to do and, oddly, his focus wasn't on sex and certainly not random sex. That had never really been his thing anyway.

He whistled as he put the steaks on the grill, dropped the lid down, and looked out at his backyard. He failed to stop and smell the roses, as they say. He was always off running to work and returning home late at night after the bar closed. But now, as he stood here at his grill, which he hadn't used in quite some time because food was available to him at the restaurant, he looked out at the view and thought it was very pretty here. Serene. He'd say serene, yes, serene.

He enjoyed the landscape for a bit longer, then turned to go back inside. As he stepped into the kitchen, Margo, fresh and clean from the shower, leaned against the door jamb, watching him. Her long, dark hair was pulled up high on top of her head. She had dug around in his drawers and found a t-shirt of his, which looked so much better on her than it ever did on him. Her tanned and sexy legs were bare and inviting. He remembered them wrapped around his waist not a half hour ago and excitement sizzled through his body. And she had the most beautiful smile on her face.

He stared for a moment.

She stared back for a couple of beats, then her lips turned up in the most beautiful smile. "You look good at the grill."

He grinned but stalked toward her, slowly. "You look good in my shirt."

As soon as he stood toe-to-toe with her, her arms wrapped around him, and her lips touched his. It wasn't a full-on kiss, but it was a slow, sweet kiss. She pulled away slightly and looked up into his eyes. He couldn't stop thinking that the crisp blue of her eyes was his new favorite color.

She smiled once again. "You felt great."

He stared at her for a long time. He grinned. "You felt better."

She chuckled and then stepped away. "What can I do to help with dinner?"

He shook his head. "Nothing. I do have a bottle of wine in the refrigerator if you'd like a glass. Maybe you could pour that. I have steaks on the grill. I have salads ready to go, and baked potatoes are in the oven. Is that going to be enough?"

She laughed. "Yes, it'll be enough. If I eat all of that I'm gonna be stuffed. I won't be able to move."

He grinned. "Well, that would be a shame if you couldn't move because I thought we could move like we did before one more time tonight."

She grinned. "Then I'll make sure not to eat too much."

His heart swelled. He liked playful Margo a lot. His timer went off on his watch. He kissed her nose, then turned around and walked outside to grab their steaks. He had a plate sitting on the table next to the grill, ready for their feast. Once he plated up their steaks, he entered the kitchen and found Margo gently bent over the table, placing their salads on their plates. His shirt was too long, dammit. He couldn't see the goods.

She looked good leaning over the table. He came up behind her. The sizzling steaks in his right hand, his left hand wrapped around her waist and pulled her against him.

"That's a sight I could get used to."

She laughed. "Well, that's good."

He kissed the back of her neck, set the plate with the steaks on the table, and held her chair out for her. "I need to give you some sustenance, so we have energy for later."

She laughed. "Well, now you're starting to have a one-track mind."

He grinned and shook his head. "No, I wouldn't say one track, but I really liked... And by that, I mean, really liked our activity earlier."

She grinned, picked up the salad dressing container, and drizzled some on her salad. She forked a helping of salad into her mouth, her soft lips moving as she chewed. He couldn't help but watch her.

"You know, Margo, one of the things I've enjoyed about you is that you eat."

She burst out laughing, covered her mouth with her hand, and finished chewing. When she calmed herself, she said, "Everyone eats."

He said, "In my business, I see it. I see first-time dates come into the restaurant, and the women will poke at their salads or only order some French fries and then only eat a couple of them because they're afraid they're gonna gain a pound. But you're just a real person. You eat, and you look fantastic."

"Well, I have to admit that over the last few years, I haven't eaten a lot. I've largely been by myself, as Logan was gone a lot. So I would eat here and there. Whatever, nothing big. I certainly never made myself a big meal. And it's just been recently, since Carley's been with me, and she likes to cook, that I've eaten regularly again." She took another forkful of salad. "I have to say, I like eating full meals. I actually feel better. Which I hadn't even realized before."

He nodded, sliced into his steak, and saw that it was done perfectly.

He was proud of himself. "I get that. If I didn't have a restaurant, I wouldn't eat full meals either. And even so, sometimes all I do is grab whatever is left over from the day or I'll have the chef make a quick little salad or something. Nothing major. It's a shame we're always on the run."

"That is a shame. You should eat better. I guess we all should. It's one of those things that we need to live, and yet we ignore or neglect when other things are going on. Doesn't really make sense, does it?

He shook his head no. "I guess it doesn't."

They finished their meal. She got up and cleaned up the dishes while he cleaned up the grill.

Afterward, he poured her another glass of wine and poured himself one. Taking her hand, he led her outside to the deck. He pulled up a deck chair for her and one for him. The chairs were side by side, facing some of his flower gardens in the back.

She sat down. He stared at her bare legs. Damn, she had great legs. Great legs. He leaned over and brushed his hand up and down her thigh.

She grinned. "That feels good."

"I have to agree with you. You're a beautiful woman, Margo."

Those crisp blue eyes sought his. "You're a handsome man, Jace Marriott." She sipped her wine. He did the same, and they sat in silence for a while, and for the first time in his life, it wasn't uncomfortable to be silent with someone. It felt good. They were both lost in their own thoughts, sitting quietly sipping wine, enjoying the pleasure of another person being there. If you wanted to speak with them, you could, but not feel the need to fill the silence. He liked it. He liked it a lot.

28

They sipped their wine and sat companionably next to each other. His landscaping was beautiful, and birds flew here and there, serenading them.

"Your gardens are gorgeous."

He chuckled. "Earlier I was thinking I don't spend enough time out here. I paid to have it all done, then forgot about it."

"That's the downside to owning a business."

He turned to her. "And living alone."

"Yeah." Since Logan took up with Sierra, he wasn't around much, and she didn't sit outside and enjoy her gardens nearly as much as she used to.

She chuckled, "I sure did have the wrong opinion of you at first."

He grinned. "I think I had the wrong opinion of you too."

She finished her glass of wine and set the empty glass on the table between them.

He asked, "Would you like another?"

She leaned forward and toward him. She glanced around the area and saw how secluded the gardens were, so she stood up and stood in front of him. She climbed on his lap, facing him, her knees were on either side of his thighs. She was able to look into his eyes, which wasn't a hardship at all. She saw him swallow a few times. His eyes never looked away from hers. His gaze was intent as he stared into hers. His hands slid up under his t-shirt, the t-shirt she wore and firmly grabbed her ass. He scooted her in so that they met in just the perfect spot. She could feel his quickly hardening cock. And it felt great. She squirmed around on top of him, feeling him grow harder. She bit her bottom lip as she stared at him. She hadn't felt so wanton in years. She practically attacked him when she walked into his house earlier today. Here she was, being the sexual aggressor once again. But it felt good to feel wanted. She could tell by looking at him he wanted her. She could tell by the way he touched her that he wanted her. And she wanted him.

She wanted him badly. She tucked her hands under his t-shirt and slid them up his ribs, pulling the t-shirt up. He lifted his arms to help her tug his shirt off; then, he did the same with hers. She hadn't put a bra on. All she had on was her little white lace panties. He bit his lip and stared at her breasts. His hands kneaded them one at a time. His tongue licked them in turn and suckled them in; then his thumbs played with the hard nipple he'd created. She closed her eyes and enjoyed him feeling her. Playing with her body. Enjoying her body.

His hands were work roughened. His fingers were firm, but he was gentle with her. She ground against him a few times, making sure he was still hard. Nothing to worry about there. He lifted hips, and she moaned as his hardness hit her clit in the best way possible. He scooted his shorts and underwear down, tugged them where they were pressed tightly together, and let them fall around his ankles. His cock was now nestled warm and hard against her clit.

His hands wrapped back around her, from behind. His firm fingers pulled her underwear to the side, baring her entrance. He lifted her slightly and slipped his dick inside of her.

It was sexy.

He gazed into her eyes, a sexy grin on his face. "Ride me, Margo."

She did without hesitation.

She moved herself up and down on him. His hands gripped her ass and helped her move. When he was ready to go faster, he urged her on. And unfortunately, she knew she wasn't going to be able to last very long. At this angle, every time she dropped down, her clit was firmly excited.

She panted hard as her need grew. He pushed his hips up higher. Just that small little bit allowed him to enter her further. And that was it. She tipped over the edge, and cried out his name as she came. He continued to move her hips quickly. Soon after, he groaned as his orgasm reached its peak.

That was fucking great. She wanted to do that again and again. With him. Only Jace.

They ended their night in his bed. He wrapped her in his arms. She lay on her left side with her right leg draped over his body. She fell asleep quickly.

The next morning, she woke to his even steady breathing. She lay still for a moment, listening to him and the sounds of the house. It was peaceful here; his breathing was calming.

He sighed heavily and tightened his arm around her. He kissed the top of her head and hugged her tightly. "Did you sleep well?"

She squeezed him, kissed his chest a couple of times, and sat up. She turned to look down at him. "I did. Did you?"

He stretched. "I haven't slept that good in a long time."

"Me either." She shook her head. "Weird, isn't it? How being with someone special changes so much in your life?"

"Yep, weird. Also, fantastic."

She smiled. "Yes, it is fantastic."

She gathered her clothes that were tossed on a chair in the corner where she'd left them yesterday. She stepped into the opulent bathroom inside his bedroom. She dressed quickly, finger-combed her hair into a bit of semblance, and rinsed her mouth. When she popped out of the bathroom, she said, "I hate to do this, but I have to go. You have a closing at 10 o'clock this morning. I have to go home and talk to Carley. We're going to go to the office and gather our paperwork for your closing. I'll see you at the title company."

He twisted his tall lanky self out of bed and stalked toward her slowly. He wrapped her head in his hands and looked down into her eyes for a long time.

"I'll be there."

He kissed her lips a few times, then stepped back.

She smiled and stepped from the room. She sighed as she descended the staircase. Maybe tonight he'd give her a tour of the whole house. She'd seen very little of it, but she'd love to see all he'd done with it.

Arriving home, she slipped in directly from the garage, and through the kitchen door. Carley waited for her at the kitchen table, a big grin on her face.

"Did you already eat breakfast?"

Margo shook her head no. Her cheeks heated. She felt like a teenager caught sneaking in far too late. She could feel the heat in her ears.

Carley smiled. "You look beautiful, Margo. Happy."

"Thank you. I feel happy. Isn't that weird?"

"No, of course it's not weird. Why would it be weird?"

"Well, when you think about it, three weeks ago I was sitting in the hospital while my husband was dying."

"Right and in those three weeks, you found out what a shithead he was, and you realized that you hadn't had a marriage in a long time. You are so ready for a good relationship. Is it a good relationship for you?"

She swallowed a big knot in her throat and looked at her sister through watery eyes. She smiled. "Oh my god. It's a good relationship. It really is. I guess I've been in denial for so long, and now it's like I've woken up or something. And he's good. He's so good, Carley. We had fun. Great conversation, and sometimes, we sat on his back deck quietly, and it wasn't uncomfortable. We both just sat and enjoyed not having to chatter."

Her sister smiled. "Good. I have breakfast here for you. Sit down. Have some coffee and then you can go shower and change and we'll go to the office."

Margo sat down at the counter shaking her head. It was almost like they were kids again. Carley was always her mother figure when their mother wasn't around. She wanted Carley to be happy too.

"Are you doing okay, Carley?"

"I am. I have some sad moments when I feel like I'm kind of the seventh wheel with your little group. Grace and Hanna are lovely. They're just lovely people to be around, and Quinn and Sid and Jace have all been very nice, but when we all go out like we did last night, I'm the odd man out. So that made me a little sad even though nobody made me feel that way. I'm just not used to being alone or single, but I'll get there."

Margo nodded. "There's a good man out there for you Carley. I just know it."

She laughed. "Well, we'll see. I'm not in any big hurry right now."

Margo nodded. "Okay, well, that's fair."

She ate the breakfast Carley had ready for her. She cleaned up her dishes and showered. They drove to the office and gathered their paperwork. She checked with Addison to see if there were any new messages and was slightly relieved there weren't any. She liked sales messages, but she didn't want Sierra's messages.

As they pulled up to the title company, she saw Jace pull up with his truck. He got out first and walked down the sidewalk toward her car. He waited at the front of her car, a grin on his face.

Margo grabbed her briefcase from the back of her SUV and sauntered up to him.

He leaned down and kissed her lips. Her cheeks heated, but she was excited to see him. He whispered, "Nice to see you."

It was sexy and low and almost like they had a secret.

She smiled. "Nice to see you too, handsome."

He turned to her sister. "Nice to see you, Carley. How are you doing?"

"I'm doing well, Jace. Thank you."

Margo strutted toward the big front door. "All right let's go get you a thrift shop, shall we?"

29

Jace left the title company with Margo and Carley close behind.

As they stepped outside, he said, "You ladies have a nice day. I'm having a little celebration at the Sandbar tonight, and Quinn, Hanna, Sid, and Grace will be there. Come and join us, please."

Margo grinned. "We'll be there, won't we Carley?"

She worried that Carley wouldn't want to come after her comment this morning about being the seventh wheel.

"Yeah," she said. "That'll be fun."

He pulled Margo into his body, wrapped her in a hug, and kissed her. She smiled beautifully, then he held her car door open. He winked as he closed her door, then jumped in his truck. He got back to the Sandbar eager for the day. It was a new day for him. Now he just had to wait till Monday night's town hall meeting. In the meantime, they had the weekend to get through with live music every day and big crowds.

He had an interview with a potential server this after-noon, and he thought maybe he would expand that to two more servers. He was going to be busy with the expansion even if the town hall wouldn't allow him to expand upward. He was going to expand outward now that he had the thrift shop taken care of. And maybe he was gonna need another bartender too. He'd take a look at that quickly, set up his ads, and go from there.

He hustled throughout the lunch hour, took care of his interviews, and felt he had a strong candidate, but he wanted to think on it a little bit. He set up the table for his friends for later tonight. He'd ordered a bigger table and had that set up over in the corner closest to the water, where the ladies liked to sit near the front row but far enough away that the music wasn't too loud. He couldn't wait for the evening to come. And actually, he couldn't wait to see Margo again. He was excited about her, about finding her. Quinn and Hanna entered the bar earlier than everyone else.

He grinned. "Our table's all set up over in the corner."

"Good to hear." Hanna looked at Quinn and winked. "I'll go on out and sit down. You guys maybe haven't had a chance to talk much lately."

Quinn watched her walk away then glanced at him. Quinn grinned. "Are you okay?"

"Man, I've never been better."

Quinn chuckled. "Good, good to hear. How are things going with Margo? She seems very friendly toward you."

"Well, if you must know, I'm very friendly toward her also."

Quinn chuckled. "All right, good to know. Glad things are working out for you man."

"They are. Things are working out great. I'm happy. She's good. We're all good."

"Excellent. Happy to hear it."

Jace grabbed their drinks, he knew what they all drank,

as any restauranteur should. They walked out to the table together. He dropped their drinks at the table and hustled inside for napkins. Grabbing a handful, he turned to step back outside when he saw Margo and Carley enter the bar.

He stopped and waited for them. He kissed Margo's lips, which felt like it had been a long time.

She smiled up at him. "Hi," she husked.

"Hi. You're a sight, as always."

"Is that good?"

"Even better."

She chuckled and he turned his attention to Carley. "Hey, Carley. Will you be drinking the Sandbar Punch?"

Carley smiled. "Hi. I sure will. Thank you."

He nodded. "Quinn and Hanna are outside at the table. Go on out and I'll get your drinks. Margo, will you be drinking wine?"

She smiled sweetly and he found himself unable to look away. "Yes. Thank you."

He winked at her, "I'll be right out."

He watched Margo as she stepped out of the door. He liked watching her walk. Actually, he liked everything about her.

He turned to Mason and saw him watching Margo and Carley walk outside. He raised his eyebrows and Mason's cheeks turned pink. "Sorry." He muttered.

Jace watched him for a moment. "Margo's mine."

Mason shook his head quickly as if to catch up on the conversation. "I wasn't looking at Margo."

Jace nodded. "Got it."

Mason took a deep breath and shook his head. "Already got the drinks, boss."

Jace grinned. Things were working out pretty well here. Mason poured the drinks and set them on a tray. He carried them out to the table, sat down next to Margo, put his arm around her chair, and relaxed back in his. He felt good. His heart felt good. His stomach wasn't knotted up over worries; he just knew somehow, deep in his gut, things were gonna work out with the town council one way or the other. Whichever way it went, he'd deal with it.

For the first time in a long time, he felt settled. He wondered about that and made a mental note to chat about it in their next Legion meeting.

Sid and Grace joined them. They'd already gotten their drinks at the bar, and they spent a few moments greeting and congratulating Jace on his new purchase.

The band began playing and the women got up to dance. That left him sitting at the table with Sid and Quinn.

Sid leaned forward. "You look happy, Jace."

He grinned at his friend, remembering that not long ago, Sid was in the same place with Grace. "I am happy. Happier than I think I've ever been."

His friend Sid grinned. "It shows."

30

Margo relaxed. The weather was gorgeous. It had cooled down a bit into the low eighties. There was a light breeze coming off the water. And the air wasn't nearly as humid as it had been.

She kicked her sandals off under the table and played in the sand with her feet. It was warm, soft, and felt good as she wiggled her toes in it.

She leaned back in her chair, Jace's arm around her back. She looked around the table at new friends, her beautiful sister, a new boyfriend, and a new life.

Hopefully, the bad shoes that had kept dropping from previously were over. She was still dealing here and there with little bouts of anger at Logan's deceit. And the nasty little things he tried to do after his death. And there'd be those thoughts for a time. If they got worse instead of better, she'd start to see a therapist.

But most of the grief stuff she'd looked up online was all just part of the process. Not the affair. Not the grabs from the company shares. None of that. Not the stolen necklace. But simply the grief at the loss of what she had from her previous life. And in her logical, wide-awake brain, what she had previously was nothing compared to what she had now. At least not relationship-wise.

She could see it now. She'd been blinded to it before. For a smart woman, she sure was dumb about some things. But she wasn't going to beat herself up about it anymore.

Her phone rang and she ignored it. Anybody who wanted to buy a house could wait for her to be available tomorrow. Tonight was about celebrating Jace's purchase. Getting to know her new friends better. And just being. That was something that, as she thought about it, she hadn't done much of over the last few years.

Her life revolved around work, work, work, work, work. It was time to take care of Margo.

Her phone rang again, and she thought how irritating it was that someone was insistent on contacting her on a Friday night.

She turned her phone over and saw it was Grant Park.

"Oh," she said, "I better take this. Please excuse me."

She stood up and walked out toward the water's edge as she answered her phone. "Hello, Grant. How can I help you?"

"Hi, Margo. I'm sorry to bother you on a Friday night, but I wanted to let you know a few things that have just come to light."

"Okay. That sounds a little scary."

"Well, not scary for you, I'm happy to report." He cleared his throat. "First of all, I've confirmed that Logan did not properly transfer any shares to Sierra. So, that worry is off the table. She's -- her attorney has already been notified of that. And through my conversation with her attorney, he made a couple of comments about some of her other lawsuits. Mostly just an innocent comment, I think, that was simply put as 'Which lawsuit is this or which case is that?'"

"Okay," she replied.

"Which had me asking Jailisa to do a little research on Miss Sierra Stigler. And she did. We found out that she's been mentioned in several lawsuits. And three of them were from former widows who she was trying to take money from. She'd had affairs apparently with their husbands, according to some of the social media posts Jailisa was able to pull up."

"No kidding! Wow!" Margo's heart raced as this news seeped in.

He continued. "And then about an hour later, Miami Sheriff's Department called me."

"Oh, dear. Why on earth is the Miami Sheriff's Department calling you?"

"Apparently, Sierra Stigler is being investigated for murder."

"Murder?" Margo gasped and put her hand to her mouth. She stared out as the water lapped the sand, changing the color from a light brown to a dark brown. It rolled over her toes, then she watched it slide back out.

"What on earth is going on, Grant?"

"Well, I just wanted to let you know that the Sheriff's Department may be contacting you to examine Logan's ashes. They might be checking for poison. They also may be asking for copies of his medical records. And they will probably be investigating his doctors and nurses, asking if any poisons had been detected in his blood system."

"Oh, my God. You think she poisoned him?"

"I don't know, Margo. I don't know. At this moment, this is just preliminary information that I've gotten. But I want you to be aware that you may be contacted by Miami police, and I don't want you to be worried about it. It's not anything against you. And if you would be so kind as to grant permission for Logan's medical records to be released so that they don't have to go through legal channels to get them, it would surely speed up the investigation."

"Of course, of course. Absolutely. Whatever they need. I will help."

"Good. Well, thank you for taking my call. I didn't want to leave this all on voicemail. I can hear music in the background, so you must be enjoying yourself. Have a have a good rest of your night. I will keep in touch with you as I find anything out."

"Thank you, Grant. Thank you so much."

Margo tapped the end call button and numbly walked back to the table with her friends. Carley leaned over and said, "Is everything all right?"

"Yes. Yes, everything is all right. Weird, but all right."

Jace had placed his arm around the back of her chair again as she sat. His hand reached around and squeezed her arm. He rubbed up and down softly. His voice next to her ear was low. "If you need to talk or if you need to leave, or whatever you need, I'm here."

She turned and looked at him. A soft smile on her face. "Do I really look bad? Everyone's asking me if I'm okay."

"You are always beautiful, but you look shocked, I guess."

She took a deep breath. "I am shocked, to be honest."

Grace sat directly across from her and smiled. "If you need to talk, we're here. And if you want to let it go. That's fine, too."

She swallowed and relayed the information Grant had just told her.

They all had the same shocked expression on their face she imagined she had on hers.

Carley said, "Unfucking believable. That woman. That fucking murderous woman."

Margo nodded. "Well, we don't know for sure, but there must be enough suspicion that she's being investigated. So, I'll allow them anything that they want for their investigation."

Carley asked, "Are you alright, Margo?"

She smiled at her sister. "I am. Just shocked at this turn of events, but if Logan had been poisoned by her, it doesn't change anything. Not for him and not for me."

She took a sip of her wine, and her hand shook slightly. She looked up at her friends, "Today's fun fact." Her friends nodded.

Jace held his glass up. "A toast."

Margo took a deep breath and held her glass up. Their friends did the same.

"New beginnings."

"Cheers."

31

As the band played their last song, he held Margo in his arms. They'd danced several times tonight, and she looked like she was genuinely enjoying herself. He knew he was.

The last chords of music played, and he whispered in her ear, "Will you come home with me?"

She pulled her head back and looked up into his eyes. "Yes."

"Good answer." He grinned.

She laughed and he spun her around a couple of times as the last note played. They walked back to the table, hand in hand. Their friends were standing to leave.

He thanked each of them for coming. "Thank you for coming and helping me celebrate ladies and gents. I sure do appreciate it. I'm looking forward to all the good things happening in the future."

He looked at Margo and winked. Her cheeks turned an adorable pink, and he thought it was stunning on her.

Sid helped Grace out of her chair, reached across, and shook his hand. "Good on you buddy, good on you."

He smiled and nodded at his friend. "It's nice that we've all found happiness, isn't it?"

"That it is bud. We've all earned it."

Sid grinned. "Fact."

Quinn came around and hugged him, then shook his hand. "Congratulations, bud. I'm looking forward to the first day we break ground."

Jace chuckled. "Me too. I'm glad you're with me on this one man."

"Me too. We're gonna build you a beautiful place."

Jace helped Margo push her chair in. "Don't worry about it. Night crew will get that."

He took her hand in his. Carley walked alongside them and the three of them skipped going inside and instead, sauntered to the parking lot directly.

Margo handed Carley her keys. "I'm going home with Jace."

Carley grinned. "Good." She hugged her sister. He watched them. They were similar in height and build. You could certainly tell they were sisters, but Margo had something that Carley didn't have, at least for him.

Carley waved to him, climbed into Margo's car, and pulled away.

Margo turned to Jace and grinned. "Are we walking?"

"We're walking." Hand in hand he led her to the path he always took from Sunset Beach Road through the copse of palm trees and to the back gate of his garden.

He unlocked the gate, let them in, and locked it behind them.

He led her through the backyard and up the back steps to the house. He couldn't wait to make love to her again. And again. And again. But probably not all tonight.

He led her through the kitchen. "Do you need anything to drink?"

"No. My god no." She laughed.

He grinned, pulled a bottle of water out of the refrigerator, unscrewed the cap, and drank half of it down.

She stood looking at him, a small smile on her face. "I'd love a tour of the house though."

"I didn't really get one yesterday."

"Well, I was remiss in not giving you a tour."

"Follow me." He walked to her and grabbed her hand. He led her around his beautiful home. He was proud of the work he had done. In some of the rooms, he had framed before pictures taken and hung them on the wall.

Margo stared at the before pictures of the formal living room. "I have to admit I didn't know what it had looked like before. I've never been in the Governor's Mansion. I'd only seen it from afar and never inside. Over time the trees and shrubs had grown up around it, and the house was barely visible from any of the roads."

"That's what I loved about it." He took her through the entire house. "You've now had a formal tour."

She chuckled. "Well, that was fantastic. You've done a beautiful job here."

"Thank you. I can't take all the credit. I hired an interior designer. Quinn did the remodel work. I just paid the bills."

She laughed. "Well, you did a great job paying the bills, and I'm sure even though somebody else was designing and doing the work, you had a lot of input about colors and furniture selection."

He laughed. "I did. I did my best."

He led her upstairs. "This is the best room of all though."

She laughed as he led her to the bedroom. He slowly undressed her. She slowly undressed him. He wasn't sure which part was the best. Her undressing him or him undressing her. Both were simply fantastic. And when they stood before each other naked, he reached forward and pulled her body close to his. He wanted to feel her skin against his. But his cock had different ideas. He lay her on the bed, crawled over the top of her, and slowly entered her. They made love. Fell asleep in each other's arms, and he couldn't imagine a better way to fall asleep.

The next morning, he got up. Margo still slept. So he snuck downstairs and made fresh coffee. He called Hanna's bakery to see if he could have cinnamon rolls delivered for breakfast.

She chuckled. "Yes, actually I just hired a delivery person to help me out with that. What time would you like them?"

He said, "As soon as you can get him here would be great."

She laughed. "They'll be right there."

She chuckled as she hung up the phone. He grinned.

Margo came into his kitchen looking wonderfully disheveled, thoroughly loved, and sexy as hell. She sauntered over, kissed his lips, and he quickly handed her a cup of coffee.

Then he took her other hand and led her out to the back deck where he had chairs set up. They sat quietly looking at his gardens.

He looked over at one point and grinned, "I have cinnamon rolls coming."

"That's wonderful, thank you," she said.

He took a sip of his coffee and then he asked, "Are we a couple?"

She turned her head. Her brows furrowed a moment, then relaxed.

She burst out laughing. "I suppose. What makes you ask that?"

"I just wondered if we were a couple. I mean we've been out on a couple of dates, but I didn't know if we were, you know, what do the kids call it these days? An item?"

"I think we're a couple." She grinned.

"Okay, that's all I wanted to know."

She laughed as she sipped at her coffee. The doorbell rang. He got up. "Cinnamon rolls."

He tipped the delivery boy, who he thought looked familiar, but he couldn't place the kid. He hustled back out to Margo and sat next to her. He opened the box and let her pick first. They silently ate their cinnamon rolls.

After they'd finished, she quietly said, "Do you want to be a couple?"

It was his turn to laugh. "Yeah, I want to be a couple with you."

"Good." She sipped her coffee again and swallowed the last of her cinnamon roll. "Because I really like mornings like this."

He grinned. "Me too."

32

Monday morning Margo was in her office at the real estate company. She was researching, preparing, and making notes.

Carley stepped in. "Good morning, what are you doing here so early?"

"Hi, I came in to do some research for Jace. I wanted to put together a list of businesses that have less than a thirty-foot buffer from the beach. Actually, two-story buildings with less than a thirty-foot buffer near the beach. In this section of town, there aren't many, but when you go down the beach past where Sid and Grace's bluff is, and Jamie Hart's barn, there's more beach along the way and there are two-story buildings over there. I wanted him to be armed with that information tonight when he goes before the Town Council.

Carley smiled at her. "Oh, you're so sweet. You really like him, huh?"

Margo stopped looking at her computer screen and folded her hands before her. "I really like him a lot, Carley. I like, I more than like him."

Carley's mouth dropped open. "Do you love him? Are you in love with him?"

She huffed a little bit and took a deep breath. "I don't know. I think so. I feel so insecure about even knowing what love is after Logan and that whole thing."

"Well don't sell yourself short. You know when you're happy. You know how you feel. Don't get knotted up over what you maybe refused to see before. And if your heart tells you that you love him, don't fight it. It doesn't come along very often, Margo."

She smiled at her sister. "Thanks, honey. I do appreciate that. How are you doing?"

"I'm doing all right. I just popped in here to tell you that I got a call and I'm going to meet a seller. I'd like to try and do it on my own. I know I don't fully have my license yet, but do you mind?"

"Not at all. I've got my phone right here. Remember to put the name, address, and contact information in the computer. It's for safety. If you don't check in after an hour, Addison will try calling you."

"I did that already. Thank you."

She patted her phone next to her. "Call me if you have any questions or you need help with anything."

"Thanks, Margo. I love you."

"I love you too, dear."

She finished her research, compiled her list, made a few copies, and her phone rang. "Margo Price."

"Hello, Mrs. Price. I'm calling you from the funeral home. Just letting you know that we just received Mr. Price's ashes back from the cremation company today, and they are here for you to pick up anytime."

She swallowed the lump that formed in her throat. Her

heart raced a little bit. That's right. His ashes. "Thank you. I appreciate it."

"You're welcome, ma'am." He hung up the phone.

She sat back in her chair and stared out the window of her office. Mixed emotions. That's how she would describe what was going on in her stomach right now. Mixed emotions. She'd been fully prepared to hate him after she found out about Sierra. And then she hated him after she found out about the shares of the company he tried to give away. Then when she saw Sierra wearing her necklace, she full-on hated this son of a bitch. But he didn't deserve to be murdered if that's what happened.

She went back to her research. She wasn't in any mood to pick up his ashes, and she thought if the police contacted her, she would just have them go pick them up. If they thought they could get useful information out of those ashes, the police could have them. Right now, her focus was on the present. She had a new life starting here, and she loved it. She looked forward to seeing Jace. They had a nice way with each other, and not that she wanted to be boring and sedate, but they both worked really hard. The down-time together was special. She looked forward to it. Who wouldn't? He was handsome. He was a business owner. He was responsible. He was reliable. He was everything that she would ever want. She just hoped she could be everything he would want.

She picked her lists off the printer, tucked them in her briefcase for tonight, and decided to go home and take a shower. Her phone rang again, and she answered it.

"Hello, Margo Price."

"Margo Price."

A chuckle came over the speaker. "Hello, Margo. My

name is Thomas. I'm selling my house, and I'd like you to list it if you don't mind."

"Oh, sure. What's a good time for me to come over and speak with you about it?"

"I'm available today. Actually, I'm available every day. I'm ready to just sell."

"Okay. I can be over in about half an hour."

"That works."

She pulled her notepad toward her. "Okay, give me your address."

He rifled off his address, and she wrote it down quickly. "All right, Thomas, I'll be there in about half an hour."

She logged on to their software and typed in her appointment along with Thomas's phone number and address. She packed up her briefcase, added her laptop, and exited the office.

She stopped at Addison's desk. "I left an appointment time on the calendar in case you need me. Carley may be calling me, or you, with help if she needs it. I do have my phone of course. And I should be back, I don't know, within an hour or maybe two. Do you need anything before I leave?"

Addison smiled. "Nope, I'm good here. I'm just pulling together documents from the title company for the closing that Logan had in the books this week."

"Thank you, Addie. I'll look that over when I get back if you want to put it in a folder on my desk. I'll go over it with Carley so she's familiar with what we're doing also."

"Sounds good."

"Have a good afternoon."

Margo left the office, jumped in her SUV, and drove to Thomas' house. She spent about an hour looking at what he had. It was a nice little house, a little ranch. It'd be good for a single person or a newly married couple, maybe a little dated, but somebody with some good design skills would be able to make it a really cute house. She was excited to list it. She worked through the listing contract with him and had him fill out the property condition report and other documents that he needed. What was included with the house and what wasn't, she told him she would get everything finalized, read through everything before she left, and then she would have him sign it electronically.

He looked over the documents and nodded. "It looks good."

She gave him the hand-held electronic document signer, and he signed his name with his finger.

On her way back home, she was excited. She was going to make this real estate company a cash cow. They were doing well, especially with Quinn's barracks. It all seemed to work really well.

She was doing what she loved with her sister. She had a new man. Life was looking good.

33

Jace walked into the town hall meeting holding Margo's hand. He saw Quinn's truck already there. And he saw Sid pulling into the parking lot as they neared the front of the building. He waited for his friend on the sidewalk.

He was nervous. He wasn't gonna lie about that. He hoped tonight would work out well. And if it didn't, if the town council could not see a two-story building on the beach, he'd still make the expansion happen. With the thrift shop gone, he would have plenty of room.

But now all he could see was a two-story building there with beautiful views from the upper deck. Sid approached, and Grace was with him. They both smiled.

Sid nodded. "Are you ready, bud?"

"I'm ready as I'm gonna be."

Margo hugged Grace. The two women smiled sweetly at each other. And Jace felt lucky.

Lucky, his friends' wives got along with Margo.

They could be a big group of friends for a long time. Until they all left this earth.

What could be better than having a strong group of friends and a woman you love? And everyone getting along? A thriving business. All of them. Quinn and Sid both had thriving businesses. Grace's little short-term rental business was doing well. She'd added two more bungalows. Hanna had her bakery. Margo had a real estate company. My god, the six of them together. They were unstoppable.

They turned and walked into the town hall meeting together.

Margo took his hand as they entered the building, and he felt great comfort from that.

She squeezed, knowing he was nervous. And gratefully, she didn't pummel him with a ton of questions.

They saw Quinn and Hanna sitting in the aisle chairs. They'd saved empty chairs next to him.

They sat down and greeted each other, and it wasn't long before the president of the board tapped his gavel to start the meeting.

They had to sit through other agenda items. The approval of last month's meeting minutes.

The treasurer's report. The agenda items for the night.

There was a dispute about dog walking.

There was a request for additional stop signs at intersections.

Both of those were denied.

And Jace was beginning to get nervous that the board wasn't in the mood to approve anything tonight.

Margo glanced up at him and smiled. She squeezed his hand. "It's gonna be alright."

He squeezed her hand in return. She had given him a list of buildings earlier that were two-story buildings along the water's edge in case he needed the argument.

Quinn was here with him with the drawings, and the architect was supposed to be somewhere in the room.

He wasn't sure. But he was as armed as he could be to present the best case he could.

His agenda item was called, and he stepped before the board where the microphone was set up.

The president said, "Please introduce yourself."

He swallowed the big knot in his throat. "My name is Jace Marriott. I own Sarge's Sandbar on the beach. I've owned the bar for two years. Since that time, I've improved it in many ways. On the outside, there wasn't a lot I could do. I painted, repaired shutters and awnings, and created a deck out back to keep the sand out of the inside. Inside, I've upgraded the kitchen equipment. I've built a business. A beautiful business. We have a stage out back. We play live music on Thursday, Friday, and Saturday nights and Sunday afternoons. We showcase local musicians. We've had one police call the entire two years I've owned the bar. That was a year and a half ago when the biker gang rolled into town and tried to cause trouble. I run a respectable business. I only hire veterans. And with my friends Sid Hoffman and Quinn Kurtz, who are also businessmen in town, we run a support group at the Legion for veterans."

"Quinn, as you know, is building housing for our veterans, and as a group, we are supporting our veteran community. This request is not only to increase the size of my bar and restaurant by knocking down the thrift shop next door, which I've recently purchased. But also to expand out that way toward where the thrift shop is now so that I can increase the size of the restaurant and kitchen inside. I'd also like to put a second story on with a wraparound deck so diners can sit up on the deck and look out at the beautiful views our waterways offer. I've got the drawings from both Quinn Kurtz of Kurtz Construction and the architect. I believe you've all been given copies of that before I came in."

"In closing, I promise the bar will be an upstanding bar kept clean and in good repair. We serve good food. We draw great clientele, and we help our veterans. I can't think of anything that is a detriment to Blossom Springs in this town that I've grown to love."

The president nodded at him, turned his head back and forth to look at the council members, and said, "Does anyone have questions for Mr. Marriott?"

A couple of the council members asked questions about the building and construction and Quinn joined him up front to answer those questions.

The board looked at Jace. The president said, "We would like to go behind doors and discuss this. If you'll please excuse us for a moment. We'll be back shortly."

He tapped the gavel and they all rose and walked to a back room.

He and Quinn took their seats with their friends.

Margo took his hands in hers. "You did great, Jace. You did beautiful."

"Thanks." He smiled at her and the nervousness that he felt from before dissipated. It just disappeared.

Quinn patted him on the back. He looked down at Sid who nodded. "Good job, bud."

And they waited. They chatted lightly to pass the time.

An older lady from the community turned to stare at them. He'd known her from previous meetings. She was usually complaining about something, and he wondered if she was about to give the board an earful about the sins of his business or something.

Her eyes dropped to his and Margo's hands, their fingers

interlocked together. She sniffed. She was a pearl clutcher from way back.

To his surprise, Grace leaned forward and addressed the woman. "Isn't it nice they've found each other? Margo's dead husband was having an affair for seven years with some whore in Miami. Poor Margo has been through so much. But Jace here, ever the hero, has made her happy again. It's that lovely?"

Margo giggled under her breath and the old woman looked into his eyes for a moment, then at Margo. She sniffed again and turned around.

Margo leaned over and took Grace's hand and squeezed. She mouthed, "Thank you."

Grace simply winked in return.

The board finally entered the room. It seemed an interminable amount of time, but in truth, when he looked at his watch, it was only about fifteen minutes.

The board sat down, recalled the meeting to order with a tap of the gavel, and the president stated so. He looked directly at Jace and said, "Mr. Marriott, will you please stand in front here?"

Jace once again walked to the microphone before the board and waited. "The board as a whole has decided to grant your two-story request. The only other improvement we would like to see is a buffer of trees between your building and the fire department. Just to add some green space since you will be expanding the hard space. The hard space that you intend to add to the ground on the first level is a little bit more than I believe..." He looked at another board member. "What was it?"

One of the other board members nodded, "Fifteen square feet."

"Yes." The president finished. "Fifteen square feet more

than the thrift shop property currently takes up, so to make up for that green space being lost, we would like trees planted at your expense to make up for that green space."

Jace nodded. "I'm happy to do that. Actually, I think it'll be beautiful, and it'll be a nice buffer between the buildings."

"Then Mr. Marriott, thank you for your contribution to Blossom Springs and this board has approved your request."

"Thank you." Jace turned and the first set of eyes he sought were Margo's.

She smiled, stood, met him halfway, and hugged him.

They quietly filtered out of the meeting as the president called the next issue to be discussed. And the second they were outside, his friends hugged and congratulated him, and his heart was full.

34

Margo stood in the conference room at the real estate office and looked over the decorations Hanna had purchased for her wedding. It was tomorrow already. Where had the week gone?

She had them organized by item: tablecloths, napkins, and vines for the arbor. Floral decorations would be delivered to the Sandbar tomorrow.

Tomorrow she'd go over with Carley in the afternoon, right after lunch, and put the flowers out on the tables and tuck them into the arbor so they wouldn't wilt before the wedding.

Then she would need time to go home, shower, change, and get ready to come back in time for the ceremony.

Hanna's best friend, Jalyn, was her maid of honor. Her parents, of course, would be there, and their friends from town.

Quinn's kids would be there, Margo hadn't met them yet. And there was a smattering of other friends here and there. Quinn had been in business for long enough that there would be plenty of business contacts and people that he associated with over time. It wasn't going to be huge, but it was going to be nice. And she was really looking forward to having a nice wedding celebration.

She started to pack up the decorations into the totes that she would transport them in, checking them off as she packed them.

The doorbell at the front door rang.

She heard Addison's voice, "Hi, how may I help you?"

"My name is Sheriff Elliott Ortiz. This is Officer Gilbert Reece. We're up here from Miami. I'd like to speak with Mrs. Margo Price, please."

Margo swallowed. She stepped out of the conference room and down the hall. As soon as she entered the entryway area, the sheriff turned.

She held out her hand. "I'm Margo Price."

He introduced himself again as he shook her hand.

She reached over and shook the hand of the deputy with him. "Would you like to come into the conference room?"

"Of course, yes."

She led them down the hall. As they entered, she said, "I have wedding supplies out here. I was just beginning to pack them up. So just give me a moment here. I'll clear some space away."

She cleaned off the decorations in front of three of the chairs so they could sit at the end.

The sheriff sat. "Are you getting married?"

She chuckled. "No, no. A friend. I'm the decorations person. So I am storing them, organizing them, and I'm responsible for getting them up tomorrow."

"Sounds fun."

"Actually, I'm really looking forward to it. How can I help you?"

The sheriff leaned forward. "I have spoken to your attorney, Grant Park, and he tells me that he has spoken to you about this. We would like to have access to your husband's medical records and his ashes. I understand he'd been cremated."

"Yes, yes. Actually, the funeral home called me a day or two ago to tell me that his ashes were available. I have not picked them up."

The sheriff nodded. "I see. Do you have a problem if we pick them up and take them to the lab for analysis?"

"Nope. I don't have a problem at all with that."

"Sounds good. We'll do that."

The deputy pulled a document from a little case that he carried. "We have a document here for you to sign showing the funeral home that we have your permission to pick up the ashes."

She quickly signed her name, slid the document back over to the deputy, and the sheriff said, "We'll get them back to you as soon as we can."

Margo shook her head and took a deep breath. "No need. Do what you want with them after you're done."

The sheriff blinked. "Look, if you're investigating Sierra Stigler then you know full well that my husband had an affair with her. Not just an affair but they've been together for seven years."

She proceeded to tell him all the things that Logan had done afterward and then she told him about the stolen necklace she saw Sierra wearing.

"So, as you can imagine, I don't want to have anything to do with my husband's ashes. Maybe Sierra would like to take them to jail with her when she goes for murder if that's indeed what happens to her."

The sheriff stared at her for a few moments. Not long.

She assumed he was probably really good at assessing people.

"I completely understand, Ms. Price. Thank you for your time."

He stood and shook her hand.

The deputy shook her hand and they both exited the office. Before they left the office, the sheriff turned to her. "Do you have documentation on the necklace?"

"Yes. I had it insured and have the paperwork on it."

The sheriff's dark eyes bore into hers. "You didn't make an insurance claim?"

Margo swallowed. "I thought about it and then leading them to Sierra. But then I received the call from Grant, and frankly..." She held her hands out and dropped them. "Frankly, I don't want the damned necklace now that she's been wearing it. I don't want the reminder. Let it be an albatross around her scrawny neck for all I care at this point."

The sheriff grinned. "I'd like the paperwork if you don't mind. Whether you decide you want the necklace or not, it could be evidence for us as to her behavior. You can decide afterward what to do with it."

He pulled a business card from his notebook and handed it to her. "If you'd email me what you have, I'd appreciate it."

She nodded. "I will do that."

The sheriff and deputy stepped from the building, and she let out a big sigh. She didn't feel bad about giving her permission. If he was indeed poisoned, it would be a shame. But she didn't do it.

And she wanted nothing to do with his ashes afterward. If she and Logan had children, maybe they would have wanted them. Logan's parents were gone. He had no siblings.

So really there was no one who wanted Logan's ashes. And she'd bet dollars to donuts Sierra Sigler didn't want them right now either. But maybe they could help bring a murderer to justice. And in his death, Logan would have to be happy with that. She wasn't willing to do much more.

Margo finished packing up the decorations and carried them out to her SUV, putting them in the back. She then got in her car and drove to the bakery. As she entered, Hanna was speaking to a customer. When the customer turned around with her cinnamon roll on a plate, Margo glanced at her and saw that she was the little old lady who had been giving her dirty looks at the town hall meeting a few days before, because she was holding Jace's hand.

Margo smiled brightly at her. "Good afternoon."

The woman froze for a moment, recognized who she was, and then nodded. "Good afternoon, Ms. Price. I hope everything is all right with you."

"Everything is wonderful. Thank you."

The lady moved on.

Margo turned to see Hanna watching her, a big smile on her face. "How can I help you?" She asked.

"I just came to tell you I've just done the inventory of your decorations. I have them packed up in totes and ready to take over to the Sandbar. I'll be stopping at the flower shop next to go over the list of items you gave me that they are supposed to have available for me and delivered tomorrow at one."

"Thank you, Margo. I appreciate all that you've done in helping me with this. Your help's been invaluable."

"Well, I don't know about invaluable, but it was fun. I'll tell you that much. And I'm happy to do it."

"Thank you. I'll see you tomorrow at one o'clock. My sister and I will be at the Sandbar setting up the decorations. You don't need to worry about a thing. We've got this covered."

"Thank you again. And thank Carley for me. I'll thank her tomorrow when I see her too."

"All right. Take care."

She walked around the end of the counter and Hanna met her there. They hugged and she felt good about her new friends. She actually had friends now.

Hanna hugged her hard and she squeezed her right back. "Thank you so much, Margo. Thank you."

Margo chuckled. "As I said, I'm happy to do it. Thank you for being a friend."

Hanna squeezed her again. She stepped back and looked into her new friend's eyes.

"Always."

35

Jace carried out the tables and put them in place. Hanna had a diagram, and he was happy to oblige.

He glanced at the diagram every so often just to make sure he was putting things where they needed to be. As he set the tables in place, Carley and Margo draped them with the tablecloths, secured the corners, and tucked the smaller bouquets of artificial flowers into each corner knot. Carley showed Margo how to fold the matching napkins to look like a rose and set them at each table setting. He enjoyed watching them work together. They chatted and laughed often. And he loved watching Margo comfortably organizing the finer details for his friends' wedding.

The flower shop van arrived, and Margo met them at the edge of the parking area. He watched her turn and point to a table at the edge without a tablecloth on it. The man nodded, and Margo was handed a large white box. She carried it to the table, and Carley hustled to the van to help. He hustled to the van to help as well.

He carried a large white box, which had some weight to

it, to the table. Margo had opened the first box and stood staring at the array of flowers in the box.

He wrapped his arms around her from behind and looked over her shoulder, which wasn't hard, he was nearly a head taller than she was.

"Those are pretty," he whispered near her ear.

"They are. This is going to be such a beautiful wedding."

He kissed her ear. "It is. You're doing a fantastic job of decorating."

She chuckled. "It's not hard with this to work with."

He chuckled. "True, that."

Marching toward the van once more he saw Carley trying to carry a crate, which looked heavy for her. "Hey, let me take that."

Carley smiled. "Thanks, Jace. It's heavier than I thought."

He hefted it to the table and peered inside. Margo glanced inside the crate. "Oh, there they are."

She gently reached inside and pulled out a small glass vase with a colorful arrangement of flowers. She set one in the center of each table. He picked up the crate and followed her. "This way you won't have to trudge back each time."

She smiled at him, and it occurred to him, he'd do anything for her if she continued to smile at him like that. Once the flowers were set on the tables, they went back to the other flowers awaiting disbursement.

Carley had an open box of small bouquets in front of her. "What are these for, Margo?"

"Ah, those are for the arbor." Margo picked up the box and moved it to the arbor. She began tucking the small bouquets into the vines. That detail brought out the effect of the arbor, and he thought the scene for his friend's wedding was spectacular. Margo finished tucking the flowers into the arbor and stood back to stare at her handiwork. He moved to stand next to her.

She smiled up at him, then turned toward the arbor. "When you stand here and see the arbor and the water behind, you can see what a gorgeous wedding this will be. In a couple of hours, while they are saying their vows, the sun will begin to set, and it's going to be magical."

"It sure is. Hanna had this vision and you've made it come to life. Bravo."

Margo laughed and he thought she was much more of a vision than the scenic one before them.

"I only added flowers. This is Hanna's vision and it's stunning."

He kissed her temple; he'd have to agree to disagree with that statement. But he was excited for his friend and the beginning of his new life. He'd been through hell with his ex, and he sure deserved this happiness he'd found now.

He was also excited about his business and the changes on the horizon.

He was excited for everything right now.

Margo was meandering around, adding flowers to the large blue pots on either side of the arbor then she tied a bow around the top. He couldn't believe how this transformed his beach bar.

He stepped back and took pictures of Margo and Carley decorating. He took pictures of the staff setting up for the buffet that would be feeding the wedding guests in a couple of hours. He snapped photos of the tables as they were fresh and clean. He got it all. He'd likely start a photo album of the various events that were held here. In the future, hopefully, there'd be many. He could offer guests some ideas. He watched Margo a moment and grinned.

He pocketed his phone and strode across the beach to

where she was now cleaning off the table that held the flower boxes. There was one large box left.

"Do you have room in the cooler for these flowers?"

"Sure. What are those for?"

She chuckled. "These are Hanna and the wedding party's flowers."

"Oh, of course. I'll find a safe place for them."

He hustled to the kitchen with the box of flowers and found a spot high on a shelf for them to rest. As he stepped back outside, the transformation of the beach and what he usually saw as he came out here, was a sharp contrast to the usual.

Margo neared, and he said, "This is stunning. I think Hanna's going to be thrilled."

Margo turned and took in the entire beach as it looked right now. "Thank you. I think it came together beautifully. I didn't pick out the colors she did, so I only get credit for putting them in place."

He chuckled. "Well, you're doing a good job with it. Even if you're being modest."

He kissed her lips lightly. When he pulled away, he looked into her eyes. His thumbs brushed her cheeks. He swallowed the lump of emotion that formed and smiled softly. "I love you, Margo."

Her eyes rounded. Then they glistened. She stared at him a moment. Her lips quivered. "I love you too, Jace. I was afraid to say it."

"I know what you mean. I was a little afraid myself. But I know in my heart how I feel. And what I feel for you is love. I love you. The time we've spent together has been the best in all my life. I look forward to each day with you. I especially like the nights," he chuckled.

She chuckled and socked him in the arm. "Okay."

He laughed. "I didn't mean I only like the nights. I meant I especially like the nights. You're a seductress. We have such-- well, what are they? Seductive nights. The thought of being with you makes me eager to come home. And the nights when I come home, and you're there waiting for me? Oh, man, do I love that. I actually think you should just move in with me so I know that you'll be home with me every night."

She swallowed but her eyes didn't veer away from his. She whispered. "Wow."

Her arms slid around his waist. "I hadn't-- I guess I hadn't thought about that."

"Margo, you'd be perfect in the Governor's Mansion, don't you think?"

She chuckled. "Oh, is that why you want me there? To be a little pretty thing in the Governor's Mansion for you?"

"No. I like you being my playmate, that's a fact. But I really want you there because I enjoy spending time with you. Think about it." He kissed her lips. "Think about moving in with me."

"I will." She took a breath. "Think about it, I mean."

He kissed her lips. Carley called out from the beach, "Come on, you two. We've got work to do."

Jace turned and laughed. "All right, all right, all right."

He kissed Margo's lips once more before sauntering back to the restaurant to bring out more of the burners for the buffet set up.

His phone rang. "Marriott."

There was a hesitation on the end and then a woman's voice. "Hi, this is Krystal Jones. I met with you earlier this week for the server position. Or the bartending position. You said both were available to me if I was interested."

He nodded. "Oh, yes, yes. Hello."

"I'm interested." She hesitated. "I mean, I'd like the job, please. I'm nervous because sometimes I shake. Remember I mentioned that. It's my PTSD."

He took a breath. "Krystal, please remember I mentioned that I only hire veterans. Also, we all have something we deal with here. My friends and I offer community discussions at our Legion here in Blossom Springs. And my friend, Quinn, is bringing in a counselor once a week to help those who need it. It's our commitment to help others."

"Yes. I remember. It's why...I mean, I'd like to be included."

"I promise you'll be included. When is your first availability?"

She cleared her throat. "I can start next week. Monday or Tuesday."

"Perfect. How about 10 o'clock next Monday? And I'll get you set up with a schedule and training."

"Thank you, Mr. Marriott."

He chuckled. "Jace. Call me Jace."

"Okay. I'll see you Monday."

"Thank you, sir."

"I'm just Jace."

"OK. Thank you, Jace."

"I look forward to seeing you on Monday. Have a great weekend."

He hung up the phone. One more thing off his plate. He stepped inside the bar.

"Mason, we have a new bartender and waitress starting on Monday. I'll have Theresa train her on Monday to wait tables and I'll have her with you on Tuesday to learn the bar. Will that work?"

"Yep. It's all good."

Margo poked her head inside. "Carley and I are leaving to shower and change. I'll see you in about an hour."

She kissed his lips, waved to Mason, and left without another word. He watched her walk out the door. His heartbeat kicked up a notch. He took a deep breath and stepped into the kitchen to check on the progress of the meal tonight; then, he'd run home and shower and change for the wedding.

~

Jace saw Margo's SUV pull into the lot as he checked the drink situation in the Tiki Bar. He strode across the beach to greet his lover.

She stepped out of the car, looking gorgeous as always, in a light blue sundress and low-heeled matching sandals. Her long dark hair flowed down her back.

She wore a blue necklace, a blue bracelet, and she carried a little blue clutch purse. She was a vision.

Carley walked around the passenger side of the car as he neared. She looked beautiful in a yellow dress, similar in fashion accessories with her necklace and her purse. The two sisters were stunning together.

He grinned as he approached them. "You two look fantastic. You're going to show up the bride."

Margo laughed. "My God, I hope not. That's not the intention of today. Let's not start fights here."

He laughed. "No fights. No fights whatsoever."

He kissed her lips. "Well, come this way. You two are seated in the second row right behind Hanna's family."

"That's wonderful. What a great spot. I'll have to thank her."

"Yep, you can do that. She called a few minutes ago to

make sure you two were up close after all the work you've done to help out."

"Aww. That's so sweet of her."

He escorted them to their seats holding Margo's hand. They stopped at the second row near the aisle.

Carley stepped in first. Margo sat on the aisle.

He kissed her lips. "I'll see you after the ceremony."

"Sounds good," she whispered back.

He then sauntered back to the bar where Quinn and Sid were waiting for him. Grace stepped out of the ladies' bathroom.

Sid held his arm out to her. "Come on, sweetheart. I'll walk you to your seat."

They exited the room and Jace turned to Quinn. "Are you excited?"

The smile on Quinn's face was huge. "I'm so excited. Thank you."

"Has Tisha been a problem?"

"Not a peep. Hanna befriended her somewhat and that has kept her out of our business."

Jace nodded. "I'm happy about that." He took a deep breath. "Are you ready to marry your girl?"

"I'm very ready."

Jace nodded. "Pastor just got here. I see his car outside."

The door opened, and the pastor stepped in. Sid entered from the back door, strode over to him, and shook hands.

Quinn did the same.

Pastor grinned. "All right, gentlemen. Are we ready to go?"

"I'm ready," Quinn said.

The three friends followed the pastor out the back door. Guests had been arriving and were being seated by the ushers, nearly every seat was filled.

The pastor glanced at Quinn, "You gentlemen, follow me, please."

They followed him to the arbor. Jace stood between Quinn and Sid, but his eyes were locked on Margo. Her eyes were locked on his. He winked at her, and her smile grew.

It affected his heartbeat speed. He hoped that would never end. She was exciting.

The band began playing the processional, and Hanna's friend, Jalyn, slowly walked down the aisle.

When she got to the arbor, she turned to their left and stood facing the aisle.

The band's volume increased, and everyone stood as the Bridal March played. Hanna began floating down the aisle with her father. Her eyes were on Quinn's.

Jace chanced a glance at Quinn and saw he was watching, a happy smile on his face.

Hanna's father stopped before him and shook Quinn's hand. "You be good to her."

"I will."

Her father turned to her and kissed her on the forehead.

"I love you, Hanna."

"I love you too, Daddy."

Her father then sat with Hanna's mother in the front row, and Hanna stepped forward toward Quinn.

The pastor said a prayer and asked them to face each other and say their vows.

Jace watched somewhat, but his eyes were always darting back toward Margo.

Hers were doing the same. He liked that. It made him feel special and loved. She'd watch him as much as their friends joining together.

The pastor said, "You may kiss the bride."

And the crowd clapped.

argo's eyes teared watching Hanna and Quinn kiss. When they pulled away, they smiled at each other. It was clear they were happy. You could see it in the way they looked at each other. And she loved that for them.

They turned toward the crowd and held their hands up high in the air. And everyone clapped and cheered for them.

The pastor then introduced them, "Ladies and gentlemen, I'd like to introduce you to Mr. Quinn and Hanna Kurtz."

The band played the recessional, and Hanna and Quinn, with smiles wide on their faces, walked down the aisle. They looked like they were floating. They smiled at their friends and family as they passed. It was nice to see them so happy.

Jace stopped next to her as he followed Hanna and Quinn down the aisle. He looked deeply into her eyes and grinned. He held his arm out to her, and she eagerly took it.

She floated down the aisle with him, eager to be next to him, touching him, with him. When they got to the back of the chairs, they were the first to greet Hanna and Quinn.

She hugged Hanna. "Congratulations, Hanna. You are a beautiful bride. You're always beautiful, but as a bride, you're more beautiful."

"Oh, Margo, thank you so much for everything that you've helped with. We appreciate it."

Margo chuckled and squeezed her once more. She then stepped up to Quinn and hugged him.

"Congratulations, Quinn. I hope you'll both be very happy."

"Thank you, Margo. We sure do appreciate it."

He squeezed her and then let her go. She turned to see Jace watching her, a sexy smile on his face. He held out his hand and she eagerly took it. They sauntered slightly away, between the chairs and the buffet area.

"You look beautiful, Margo. I couldn't stop staring at you."

She chuckled. "I kind of felt the same way. I wanted to watch the wedding. I truly did. But I couldn't stop looking at you. You're very handsome."

He chuckled. "Well, thank you. I'm lucky to have you with me."

The band started to play slow, soft music, as the guests congratulated the bride and groom.

Jace pulled Margo close and swayed to the music. She eagerly swayed with him. Wrapping her arms around his neck, she looked up into his eyes. "I enjoy dancing with you. I've never really been much of a dancer, but you're a great dancer and you make me feel like I want to do better."

He chuckled. "I've always liked dancing, but I only like it when I have a great partner. I enjoy dancing with you, Margo."

Her heartbeat skipped. Butterflies fluttered around in her

belly. She was falling like crazy for this man. Was that nuts after what she'd just been through? What was she thinking getting involved so quickly after all that she'd been through? But then again, even she recognized that she hadn't really been in a relationship for a long time. It was a stagnated half-relationship at best. But her gut told her Jace would never cheat on her. Jace was not Logan. And she was grateful for that. And she was also willing to let go of the things that made her angry with Logan.

She was so sure this was the relationship she'd always wanted. This is how she wanted to be treated. With grace and love with a man who looked at her with love in his eyes. She couldn't get that if she closed herself off from love ever again. She didn't want to do that. And she loved Jace. It was too late to pull anything back; she'd already let her heart love. Probably because he was easy to love.

She watched Quinn and Hanna get married, and all she could think about was how lovely it was when two people truly wanted to be together. To be in love and to have your one true friend, who you enjoyed spending every day with. Talking to at the end of the day and first thing in the morning. Spending time with, in her case, maybe building a business. Dinner with friends, events with family, everything. Spending time with them. That's what she'd always wanted. And when she looked at it now, she didn't really ever have that with Logan.

She was dumb to think what she had with Logan was a marriage. It wasn't a marriage at all. At first, they enjoyed traveling together, but then he enjoyed traveling with someone else.

The music stopped, but Jace didn't let her go. They continued to sway back and forth slowly in the sand. Her heart felt full and happy, and...at peace.

Finally, Jace lifted his head and looked into her eyes. "That was really nice."

She smiled. "It was. I'd like several more of those this evening, please."

His smile was beautiful. "You got it. How about we start each day with a dance and end it that way too?"

Her heart swelled and her body tingled. "I'd like that more than I can ever express."

He chuckled, wrapped his arms around her again, and spun her slowly around. When he let her go, he winked at her. That was sexy.

Then he grinned. "How are we going to do that, Margo?"

She swallowed but stared deeply into his eyes. "I'm moving in with you, Jace. That's how we'll do that."

The smile that he bestowed on her was magnetic. It was without a doubt the sexiest smile she'd ever seen on any human in the history of the world.

"I like that more than I can ever express."

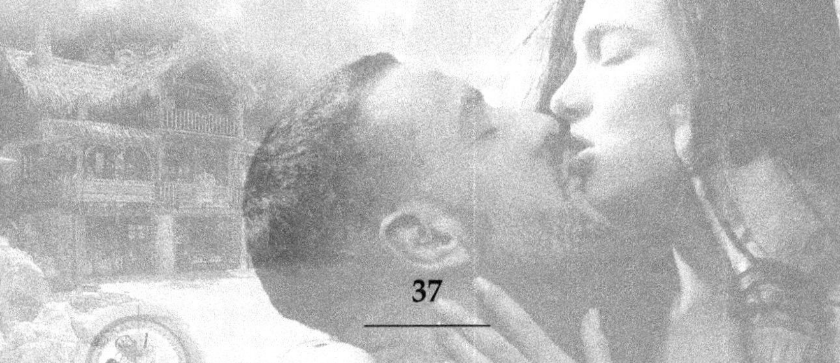

37

Throughout the evening, Jace danced with Margo often. He enjoyed dancing with her, and he had to admit, it was nice being off work even though he was literally at work. But it was nice being able to set aside his business head for a while and focus on his friends and his new relationship with Margo. As they danced, her phone rang. She chuckled.

Her phone was in her dress pocket. He stopped dancing as her phone continued to vibrate between them. "I'm not working tonight so we can just let it go to voicemail."

"Are you sure?"

She smiled. "Yes, I'm sure."

He wrapped his arms around her once more and swayed to the music, but her phone continued to vibrate.

He chuckled. "Go ahead and take it. I'll just wait right here with you."

She took a deep breath as she pulled her phone from her pocket. "Margo Price."

As she listened, her expression changed. Her smile

disappeared. Her brows furrowed and he worried it was bad news. He waited near her, to be her support if she needed it.

"What kind of poison?"

Jace watched her face as the news filled her ear.

When she said, "Okay, well thank you for letting me know and yes, you have my permission."

She pocketed her phone and looked up into his eyes. He whispered, "Are you alright?"

"Miami police have arrested Sierra Stigler for murder."

"Are you kidding me?"

"No, I'm not kidding you. They have arrested her for the murder of two men in Miami. And, he said they've searched her home and believe she poisoned Logan. They are hoping the lab can get enough evidence from his remains to prove that. She used an older poison called Thallium. It's tasteless and odorless and takes a while to build up in the system. By the time Logan went to the doctor, he was suffering organ failure."

He bent his knees and looked into her eyes. "How are you feeling? Are you alright?"

She nodded slowly and shrugged her shoulders. "It doesn't change anything in my situation, Jace. Logan had an affair with her for years. He betrayed me. He lied to me. He cheated on me. It doesn't change anything as far as that part of my life goes."

He pulled her in his arms and hugged her tightly. "I'm so sorry, Margo. You don't deserve anything like that."

She squeezed him tightly and he could feel how fast her heart was beating. She looked up at him. "You know, even if Logan was poisoned, he's still dead. So it doesn't change anything."

"Right, of course not." He hugged her again. His hands

smoothed over her back. "I'm very sorry that you still have to go through these surprises."

She looked up at him. "If you're sorry for anything, be sorry that Logan was a dumbass."

He chuckled. "Well, he was a dumbass, but I won't be sorry for that because that brought you to me. I'm not sorry for that at all."

Her eyes glistened and he saw her swallow a few times. "I'm not sorry about that either. Should we go sit down somewhere and just have a drink?"

"Sure."

He led her to a table, and they sat down. Sid and Grace joined them soon after. Margo explained about the phone call, and both Sid and Grace looked like deer caught in the headlights.

Grace finally said, "Holy crap! What a weird, weird situation."

Margo nodded. "I know. Never dreamed I'd be going through anything like this."

"Well, that's a fact." Grace sighed. "Oh, my goodness." She reached across the table and squeezed Margo's hand. "Do you need anything?"

Margo's smile was soft. She looked around the table. She reached over and took his hand in hers. She continued to hold Grace's, and she said, "Actually, I have everything I need right here. I have good friends. My sisters are close by or here with me, and I have this man right here."

His heart grew so fast he thought it was gonna burst out of his chest. He leaned over and kissed her softly.

"Always," he whispered.

They enjoyed their drinks. Hanna and Quinn joined them for a little while, but they had guests to speak to.

Carley joined their table after a while. She smiled brightly at the group. "I just got my first listing on my own."

Margo grinned at her sister. "That's wonderful Carley, but until the contract is signed, you don't have a listing."

Carley nodded. "I know. But I have an appointment for tomorrow morning."

Margo hugged her sister. "Congratulations."

"And..." Carley continued. "I have applied to school to get my license."

Margo started at her a moment. "You really like the real estate business?"

Carley's smile said it all. "I love it."

He raised his glass for a toast. "Here's to Carley and her new career."

Jace woke with Margo's naked body snuggled next to him. He stared at the coffered ceiling for a few moments, wondering at all that had taken place in just a few short weeks. They'd partied with Quinn, Hanna, and company until nearly two this morning. He had new staff starting soon. His expansion was in the works. Bulldozing would start Monday on the old thrift store. The architect was drawing up the building plans and within three or four months, his expansion would be complete.

But the best part of his new life was sleeping next to him. He felt calmer with Margo. More grounded. He just knew things would work out with the town council, and he credited her with that. He loved her sense of humor, and he loved how she dealt with tragedy. She was grace and beauty personified. Witnessing her dealing with such turmoil in her life made him want to be better.

She sighed and stretched. He rolled onto her, his elbows holding him up. He grinned as he stared at her sleepy eyes.

"Good morning. Did you sleep well?"

She mumbled, "Yes. Did you?"

"I did." He kissed her lips, her cheeks, then her jawline to her ears, down her neck, and then back up. "Do you want to play hooky today?"

She smiled. "What kind of hooky?"

"I thought we'd go boating."

"Boating? It sounds wonderful but I didn't know you had a boat."

He chuckled. "I don't, but I have friends who do. I actually have a friend with a sailboat, and he said he'll captain for us today while we relax and enjoy the weather. Good food, great company, warm weather, quiet seas, how about that?"

"That sounds fantastic." Her hands cupped his face, and she kissed his lips a few times.

"I'll need to let Carley know and see if she is comfortable managing things today. There isn't much to do except the closing from Logan's buyer. But all she has to do for that is show up at the closing and take the check for our fee."

"Okay. I need to contact Mason and let him know I won't be around. See if he'll keep the place going in my absence."

She chuckled. "A day off for business owners isn't really a day off, is it?"

"Not in the true sense of things. And tonight, I'll need to be back because we have music, and we'll need the manpower."

"Is there anything I can do there?"

He pulled back and stared at her. "You mean work?"

"Yeah. I can help you."

"Like what? What would you want to do?"

She shrugged. "I can hostess. I used to do it back in the day."

His brows shot up. "I don't want to make you work on your time off."

"Well, what would I do? Sit here and wait for you? Carley is leaving this afternoon to pack up some of her things at the house. So, I'll be sitting home alone, or here."

"You could pack up your things and move them here."

She laughed. "I could do that, but not at night. Let me work with you."

He kissed her again. His heart was swelling. "Okay. Then, tomorrow, you and I will go and move some of your things here."

"Okay. I thought I'd let Carley live in the house and if she wants to buy it when her house sells, I'll make her a great deal."

"I love the way that sounds."

He kissed her again, this time, it was sensual. Her lips were soft and pliable as his lips molded to them. He licked her lips, and she opened hers to let him in. Their tongues danced and swirled together. His cock thickened and hardened, and she wiggled her hips and spread her legs. Damn, she was sexy. Her hands roamed his body, sliding sensually down his back and squeezed his ass. She pulled him to her, and he wasn't going to let the moment pass.

Lifting his hips, his cock found her entrance and he slowly slid inside of her. He'd never tire of that feeling. Her warmth wrapped around him snuggly, her wetness spoke of her desire and when he moved in and out, her body matched his rhythm move for move. Much like they moved together on the dance floor, they moved together perfectly when they made love.

He looked into her eyes, his new favorite color of blue.

She stared into his eyes, and he could see her love. It was real and sincere, and he'd never felt this level of love and passion in his entire existence. Man, he'd been missing out on this for years.

His hips continued to pull out and push in. Her hips continued their dance. Together it was bliss. The look on her face was exquisite. That moment when the pain mixed with pleasure as her orgasm built and the urgency to reach the pinnacle was stunning. Her fingers tightened on his ass, and when she tumbled over the edge of ecstasy, she called out his name. That was the best.

He stared at her a moment, then increased his pace as his orgasm tightened his balls and thickened his cock. The moment he came he stiffened and jerked, each feeling intensified as he emptied himself into her.

This must be what heaven felt like.

38

Margo finished showering. She opted to put her hair up in a knot on top of her head today. Being out on the water would have it blowing around too much and it would be in the way. She'd run home and put on shorts and a tank top after she spoke with Carley.

She descended the grand staircase and grinned. She was going to live here with a man she adored. Who knew so many things would change in a month's time?

When she stepped into the kitchen, Jace stood at the stove wearing a pair of shorts and a tank top, making something that smelled heavenly.

He looked up when she entered, and his smile was immediate.

Setting the spoon he stirred his omelet with on a spoon rest, he wrapped her in his arms and spun her around.

"We dance every day," he whispered near her ear.

She folded her arms around his shoulders and pressed her body tightly to his as he led them in a seductive dance around the kitchen. His right hand smoothed down her back and pulled her ass to his body, then he spun them again.

She laughed as their dance continued. He chuckled in her ear, and then she heard his sigh, and it made her heart swell. He was content right now.

He spun her once more, then stopped and kissed her lips. "I poured you a cup of coffee when I heard the shower shut off. Take a seat at the table and I'll finish breakfast."

"You'll spoil me."

His lips turned up into a sexy grin. "I'm happy to do so."

She sat at the table, in front of her coffee cup and sipped at the warm liquid. She looked out the windows to the gardens outside and a peace settled over her.

Jace brought her plate to the table. "A messy omelet, madam."

She laughed as he set both of their plates on the table and sat across from her. She took a bite of his omelet, and it was delicious.

She took a deep breath as she swallowed her last bite and sat back in her chair. She sipped her coffee and stared at this beautiful man across from her.

"Do you remember a while ago you asked me what it would look like for me to feel happy and content again?"

"Yes."

He set his fork on his empty plate and pushed his plate to the middle of the table. He stared at her quietly waiting for her to finish. Emotions rushed into her body and her nose tingled as tears threatened. She swallowed. "It looks like this."

A tear spilled from her eye and slid down her cheek. He reached over and swiped it away with his thumb. His eyes glistened and he sniffed a couple of times. She saw his Adam's apple bob as he swallowed repeatedly.

"It does for me too." He finally managed.

She took a deep breath and held it before releasing it. She was a different person these days. Old Margo would never have played hooky or danced in the kitchen. New Margo savored all of this and more.

Margo took Jace's proffered hand and stepped onto the boat. He guided her to the back of the large sailboat where there was a beautiful sitting area.

White sofas lined the entire back of the boat. Tables made of teak wood, and adorned with floral arrangements, stood in front of the sofas and the view over the back of the boat into the water was spectacular. Jace held her hand and directed her to the middle of the sofa. He seated himself next to her and wrapped his arm around the back of the sofa behind her, his hand caressing her arm soothingly.

A man, who wore white pants, a white shirt, and a captain's hat, walked toward them. He smiled at her and nodded his head. "Ms. Price, my name is Anthony, and I am your captain today."

She smiled at his politeness. "It's nice to meet you, Anthony. Thank you for allowing us the use of your boat and for leading us on this journey."

He grinned and nodded. Jace stood and the two men shook hands. "Thank you for today, Anthony."

Anthony nodded, and it seemed as though he had become emotional. He took a deep breath. "Thank you for all you've done to help me."

Jace nodded. "Any time."

Anthony nodded to her once more and Jace took his

seat. "We'll be pulling away from the dock in five minutes. Please sit back and relax."

She smiled again. "Thank you."

A waiter brought them out a beautifully arranged plate of fruit and cheeses. He set them on the table, without a word, then disappeared quietly.

The sails were hoisted. She'd never seen anything like that in her life and the thrill that ran through her experiencing it now was exciting. They slowly pulled away from the dock.

Jace once again put his arm around her, and they both closed their eyes and turned their faces to the sun. It was wonderful. Simply wonderful. When had she ever had a moment to just sit and enjoy the beautiful weather here in Florida? Her life consisted of working on beautiful days like this.

After they were out on the open water, Jace pulled a bottle of champagne from a cooler, which looked exactly like the sofa. She hadn't noticed it when they arrived. She chuckled. He opened the bottle, the cork popping out with its usual *pop,* and she laughed. He pulled beautiful crystal champagne flutes from inside the same cooler and poured them each a glass of champagne.

She admired him as he set about making this a lovely day off for both of them. His tanned skin and strong arms were bare in his tank top. His muscular legs were sexy in the shorts he wore, and he had sandals on his feet, which he'd already kicked off.

He handed her a champagne flute. "Here's to us."

She smiled. "To us?"

He pulled a gorgeous, long-stemmed red rose from the vase in front of them and handed it to her. She smiled and smelled the rose, then looked into his eyes. "I meant what I said earlier today, you'll spoil me."

When he smiled at her it nearly took her breath away. "I hope so."

They sipped their champagne, then he set his flute on the table before them. He stared into her eyes for a long time, then dropped to one knee in front of her and pulled a ring from the pocket in his shorts. Her heartbeat increased so much she could hear the beating in her ears. She stared at his handsome face as he smiled at her. He held the ring up, the sunlight glinted off the diamond and sparkled beyond belief.

"Margo Price, will you marry me so I can spoil you forever?"

She swallowed the emotion that filled her throat. The visage before her of her handsome man and the ring he offered her as a symbol of his love wavered as tears filled her eyes.

She didn't have to think about this decision. She knew this morning when she confessed that she felt happy and whole, that he was her person. "Yes. I plan to spoil you too."

His smile grew. "All that matters is that we dance, spend time, and enjoy each other. Always."

He slid the gorgeous sparkler on her finger. He then rose and kissed her lips, and she kissed him right back.

EPILOGUE

JACE

Jace stepped into the office he now shared with Margo. She stood in front of her desk with stacks of goodies she'd ordered for the Sandbar.

She turned when he entered, and her smile was huge. "Look, the tablecloths have come in."

The bright blues, yellows, and greens were beautiful. She turned to the next box, sliced it open with her box cutter, pulled the colorful plastic margarita glasses from the individual compartments, and set them out on the table. The colorful stems of the glasses were a variety of parrots, surfboards, and flip-flops. They matched her tablecloths.

"Look at these. Aren't they fabulous?"

He chuckled. "They are indeed."

"This is going to be the event of the year."

"I have no doubt. You do an amazing job with all of our events."

She turned and smiled. "Thank you. I'm so happy with how they look together. I also have napkins to match, and for the Sandbar Punch, I bought these cute little mason jars with handles on them." She held them up for effect.

Jace looked into her eyes and chuckled. "Those are wonderful."

He kissed her lips. "Now it seems you have everything set for the grand opening, but what about our wedding?"

She set the mason jar glass on the table and turned to look at him. "What do you want for the wedding? If we have it here, we'll essentially be working. And so will the staff. We wanted everyone to have a great time and not have to work."

He grinned and leaned his butt against his desk on the other side of the room. "I'm glad you asked. I found a company that will come in and work the restaurant for the night. They bring waitstaff, cooks, bartenders, all of it. Since we won't be collecting cash, there's no money to worry about. All we have to do is work with them the day before for a couple of hours and show them where everything is. We can have Marco work with the kitchen staff. Mason can work with the bartenders. Theresa can work with the wait-staff. Then, everyone can be here and enjoy themselves."

"Really?" She leaned her butt against her desk and stared at her handsome future husband. "You've really been working on this."

"I have. Because I want you to be my wife. We've been engaged for five months now. I don't want to wait anymore. You've already moved in with me, sold your house to Carley, and you've sold your real estate business to her as well. You've joined me here at the restaurant and business has never been better. Now, it's time to focus on us."

She grinned and sauntered across the office toward him. He reached out when she was close enough, grabbed her by the waist, and pulled her to him. Her arms quickly wrapped around his shoulders. He kissed her lips. Softly at first, but their kiss deepened. When they pulled apart for air, he smiled and stared into her eyes.

"Set the date, Margo."

She smiled. "Next week, Saturday?"

He chuckled. "That's only eight days away."

"You said you wanted me to set the date."

"I absolutely do. But I also thought we had a birthday party scheduled here."

Her fingers slid into his hair and rotated slowly. He loved the way she massaged his head like this. She tilted her head slightly. "They canceled. Something to do with a family argument or something."

"When did this happen?"

"A few days ago."

"You didn't mention it."

Her lips turned up into a sweet smile. "Because I was doing some planning of my own. I wanted to make sure things could happen for us. Hanna can make a cake. I didn't tell her it was for us. She thinks it's for a party here. My sisters are available to be here. And I was sly when I asked Grace and Hanna if they had any plans for next weekend so they would be here. Also, I managed to find a dress yesterday, so we're actually all set now."

"You did all this planning without telling me?"

She laughed, and he couldn't look away from her. She was radiant. "You've been asking me to set a date for a while. And, with the expansion, my move, and training Carley in the real estate company, there's been no time for us. I thought you'd be happy if I took all the steps I needed, to make sure the date would work."

He kissed her again, then wrapped his arms tighter around her and moved them away from the desk. He swayed with her, dancing slowly and he enjoyed the feel of her body so close to his. Her fingers still massaged his head, her body touched his in the most delicious places and he was an incredibly happy man.

"I'll see if I can get them on short notice," he whispered.

She giggled. "That was the last piece of the puzzle."

He twirled them around a couple more times, then stopped dancing and kissed her again. They stood still, holding each other for a few moments, each of them grounded the other. They'd marveled about that recently. Their lives naturally joined together in all things. Business and personal. It all came together.

He bent and rested his forehead against hers for a moment, then stood back. "Thank you for that reprieve. Now, are we all ready for the Grand Opening tomorrow night?"

"Yes, this was the last of the supplies. I wish it would have come sooner, but at least they're here now. I'll take the glasses to the kitchen and get them washed."

"Perfect. Jami Hart called, and they're home now and will be here to set up around noon tomorrow."

"That's great. I'm glad they made it home. They've been on tour for a while."

"Yeah, they're really hitting it big."

"I'm going to place a call and see if that company can fit us in next Saturday. Do you want to get married in the afternoon or evening?"

"The evening. Wasn't it beautiful when Quinn and Hanna married in the evening?"

"It was beautiful. Yes."

"Are you okay with that?"

He chuckled. "Yes. I'm fine with that."

She smiled and nodded her head. "I'll make some calls too and let everyone know we're getting married next week."

He swatted her butt, then turned to pick up the notebook he'd written the company name and phone number down in. They'd be his first call.

She winked at him as she carried the boxes of glasses to the kitchen. He was getting married next week, and he couldn't wait.

~

Margo

Margo put the final tablecloth on a table and glanced around at the colorful display. She loved standing up here on the upper deck. The view was impressive. They'd have to get some wedding pictures from up here next week.

She'd found cute little pineapple centerpieces for each table, and looking over them all now, they were perfect. From the upper deck, she could see the newly built floating deck downstairs, which eliminated the raking of the sand and chairs sticking in the sand at the tables. Everything was much cleaner, and their business had grown so much with the expansion. They were fortunate.

Heading downstairs, she checked on the tables down there, then checked the new menus that had arrived yesterday to make sure they were nestled in the hostess stand.

The grand opening was to begin in a half hour. She was nervous but also excited because it was a coming out of sorts. Many folks in town still didn't know she'd sold the real estate company to Carley. It had been Price Realty, but today was the first day that Carley changed the name on it to Florida Realty. She had done a fantastic job learning the business. She'd gotten her license and taken over the office quickly, and all of it seemed natural to all of them when Margo decided if she was going to start a new life, she needed to get rid of her old life. Her house, her business - all of it. It had begun to feel like a weight around her neck. When she began helping Jace on the weekends at the Sandbar, she found she enjoyed it so much. She loved working with him. And she was good at it.

Jace strutted across the floor of the restaurant, a sexy grin on his face. "Are you all set?"

"I am. Are you?"

"I am." His grin widened. "Come in the kitchen and eat something with me."

She lay a hand over her belly. "Oh, I'm not..."

"Come and eat something with me." He pulled her by the hand to the kitchen. She clung to his hand tightly, and as they entered the kitchen together, she noticed their staff standing there looking at them.

Marcus counted, "One. Two. Three."

They all yelled, "Surprise."

There was a cake in the center of the stainless-steel table that said *Grand Opening* and *Welcome.*

She couldn't think of anything to say. She smiled and looked at Jace. "I don't understand."

Jace looked at Theresa, who took a step forward. "We wanted to formally welcome you to the Sandbar. You've joined us and immediately began working, and we haven't had the opportunity to formally tell you how happy we are you're here." She shrugged. "Oh, and it's our grand opening, and we're all pretty excited."

Margo laughed and hugged Theresa. "Thank you so much." She looked at the others. "Thank you all so much. You've made this transition wonderful."

They clapped, and Marcus cleared his throat. "Can we eat the cake now?"

Jace laughed. "Yes. Eat the cake. Save us a piece."

Marcus laughed. "You two should take the first pieces."

He cut the cake and plated them each a piece. They all dug into their cake and laughed and chatted. Jace whistled to quiet everyone down, then said. "We have an announcement for you all."

They stopped talking and stared at them. Jace looked into her eyes, a beautiful grin on his face. "We're getting married next Saturday, right here. You all are invited and won't have to work."

There was a smattering of claps and some questions, and Jace patiently explained how it would all work. As he finished, the doorbell rang, and Margo nodded. "That's me. We're up."

She strode out to the restaurant and found a younger couple at the hostess stand waiting. "Welcome to Sarge's Sandbar. Would you like to eat inside or outside?"

The young man said, "Actually, can we eat upstairs?"

Margo smiled, "You sure can. Follow me."

Their evening passed in a whirl. They were a full house most of the night. The music was fantastic, and the energy was high. Some of that may have been from the cake, but the staff was happy and so proud of the restaurant and bar area.

Her sisters, Carley, Holly, and Josseline, had come to celebrate with them. Holly and Josseline were staying at Carley's this week and would be here to help her get ready for their wedding.

A couple of times during the night, she thought she saw Mason staring at Carley, but when he saw her watching him, he busied himself. She'd have to ask Jace about it later.

~

One week later...

Margo dressed in her wedding gown. It was a tea-length silver gown. She didn't want to wear white. And as she shopped, she saw this one in the store window and fell instantly in love with it. She had her hair piled high, a few dark tendrils trailed down, and white roses were tucked in here and there. As she looked in the mirror now, she was completely and totally happy with how she looked.

Jace was getting ready at Sid's place, and they'd be down here in about a half hour.

Her sisters were getting ready in the various guest bedrooms here in the governor's mansion. She still couldn't believe she lived here. She stepped out of her bedroom and started down the stairs when Carley stepped from her room. "Hey."

Margo stopped and looked at her sister. "You look absolutely beautiful, Margo."

She smiled. "Thank you, Carley. You look beautiful, too."

Her sisters were wearing different colors. Carley wore a soft pink tea-length dress. Holly wore a light blue tea-length dress. And Josseline, the only sister with light brown hair, wore a light green tea-length dress. They all wore matching shoes. She'd purchased each of them a single diamond necklace with a gold chain. They were simple, elegant, and perfect. She'd used the money she'd earned from selling off the necklace Logan had stolen and given to Sierra. It was the perfect use for the money, and her sisters were overwhelmed and happy with the gifts.

She stood at the top of the steps with Carley as her sisters stepped from their guest rooms one by one. They stood together, holding hands in a circle. Margo glanced at her gorgeous sisters and smiled. "Thank you all for being here with Jace and me today. It is, without a doubt, the happiest day of my life."

Josseline sniffed and Carley said, "Nope. No tears. Let's go get a new brother-in-law."

The women walked the path from the Governor's Mansion to the Sandbar. A few cars were already in the lot, waiting for the wedding to start. They entered from the back and slipped into the office. A knock on the door had Carley telling her to hide behind the door in case it was Jace.

Margo laughed but did as her sister asked. It was the photographer asking to take some pictures.

They dutifully obliged, and then Grace found them on the upper deck. "It's time to get married, Margo. Jace is pacing downstairs."

Margo smiled. "I'm ready. So very ready."

She stood inside the restaurant as her sisters each walked up the aisle. Jami Hart sang a soft, pretty rendition of "Faithfully" to serenade them. It was beautiful.

She stepped from the restaurant and to the end of the aisle, and Jami started singing "Heavenly" by Bryan Adams, one of her favorites. She walked down the aisle toward Jace, who had to swipe a couple of tears from his cheeks. It was hard for her not to cry when he was emotional. But she made it.

As they stood face to face, she smiled at her handsome, almost-husband, "You're crying. This is supposed to be a happy day."

He chuckled. "I've never been happier. Never."

The pastor cleared his throat lightly, and they turned to face him. He prayed with them, and he spoke of love and fidelity and marriage as a partnership. He mentioned communication and understanding. And, finally, since he knew them well, he told them to make sure they danced every day. They both agreed. Their vows were said. Rings exchanged. And finally, the kiss.

Jace held her head between his hands and stared into her eyes for a long time. She loved looking into his eyes. It was her new favorite color of brown. He whispered. "I love you, Margo Marriott."

She smiled at him. "I love you, Jace Marriott."

Finally, he kissed her. And it was beautiful. She remembered their friends and employees clapping and cheering for them. But all she had her mind focused on was Jace.

The pastor then said, "Ladies and gentlemen. I'm proud to introduce you to Mr. & Mrs. Jace and Margo Marriott."

Mason is about to find out what he's really made of. Find out right along with Mason is *Sensual Nights* https://geni.us/SensualEBPJF

Or, turn the page to get to know **Mason Thompson,** bartender extraordinaire, and Jace's right hand at the Sandbar. Mason's story is complex and he's far more than your average Joe. But, he's seen too many things and it's messed with him - body and soul.

BONUS EPILOGUE

Meet Dr. Mason Thompson, the enigmatic hero of *Sensual Nights*. You may remember him as the bartender at Sarge's Sandbar in this story, *Seductive Nights*, but there's so much more beneath the surface. Once a skilled trauma surgeon in the US Military and later in the private sector, Mason's life took a dramatic turn that led him to the quiet town of Blossom Springs. What could drive a man from saving lives in the operating room to pouring drinks in a small-town bar?

Dive into Mason's story to uncover the heartbreak, the trauma, and the passion that reshaped his world. You won't want to miss it.

A call came into the hospital via the helicopter response team.

"We have a gunshot victim coming in five. Need trauma team activation; severe blood loss, massive trauma."

The operator receiving the call replied, "On it."

She immediately pressed the button on her phone to the trauma team. "Incoming gunshot patient, severe blood loss. Doctor Thompson and all surgical staff report to OR two."

Mason hurried from the doctor's lounge and jogged down the corridor to operating room two. His heart raced, and the adrenaline immediately pumped through his body. The outside door crashed open as he put on his rubber gloves. Dashing to the gurney as they wheeled it into the OR, he yelled. "Report."

"Airway restriction. Administered one thousand ccs of isotonic solution to maintain BP. Tranexamic Acid administered to reduce blood loss. Heavy compression on wound. Transport was only ten minutes, not enough time for anything else."

Mason took a deep breath and stared down at the man lying on the gurney. How many hundreds just like him had he seen? How many of them didn't make it? Sweat beaded on his forehead and rolled down his back. His breathing came in spurts, and his vision dimmed slightly. He mumbled to himself, "Hang on."

He shook his head quickly to get it back in the game. "I need two thousand cc's of Lactates Ringer's. Get his BP. Intubation tray stat. Send for blood." He swallowed. "Type?"

"O-negative," someone called out.

A scalpel was pressed to his hand. He kneaded the man's throat with his fingers, found the perfect spot, and pressed his scalpel to it to open his trachea. He made quick work of inserting the tube, and the whoosh of air dispelled from the man's body also brought with it blood. His vision dimmed again as the scurrying of medical professionals around him faded. He continued to sweat profusely, his hands shook, and he needed to get out of there.

"Doctor?"

He turned toward the voice. An intern he'd been working with in the hospital stared at him. Brows furrowed. Mason growled. "Take over, stat."

He stepped away as the intern replaced him. He made his way to the scrub room and sat on the stainless bench near the wall. He absently pulled his gloves off and tossed them in the wastebasket. He bent over to put his head between his knees. He had to get out of here. He was a hindrance at this point in his career.

All the young men and women he'd seen on the battlefield in Afghanistan came to haunt him every night in his dreams. Actually nightmares. Especially those he couldn't help. The blank stares on the battered faces haunted him. Another life lost in a war on foreign soil. How many more?

His heart squeezed, and his breathing shallowed. He couldn't seem to get his lungs to take in a full breath. "Hey." A soft voice somewhere near him called.

He swallowed and tried to even his breathing out. It took everything he had in him to regulate himself. His breathing, his heart rate, sweating, and shaking. He closed his eyes tighter and inhaled a deep breath and held it. After a moment, he let it out slowly. He repeated this several times.

"Hey, Mason," the voice called again. He lifted his head and saw the young intern he'd turned his patient over to so unprofessionally.

His voice was dry and gravelly when he responded, "How did it go?"

"He's stable."

Mason nodded his head. "Thank you."

The intern, what was his name again? It didn't come to him just now, sat on the bench next to him. "How are you?"

Mason sucked in another deep breath. "I'm not good here. I have to leave."

"Yes. Maybe tomorrow you'll feel better after some rest."

"No." He cleared his throat. "I'm not good here. I'm not good for anyone here. I had a panic attack with a patient on the table."

The intern sat quietly for a moment. After a lengthy silence, he asked, "Are you seeing a counselor?"

"No."

He sat up straighter and turned to face him. "You need to. There's no shame in asking for help. It's actually the least shameless thing you can do. Getting healthy again is good for you. It's also good for the people around you. With your training and experience, you can help so many people. But you need to be healthy to do it."

He held out a small rectangular business card. "This is who I see. He's very good. Please call him."

Mason swallowed the dry lump in his throat and gently took the card held out to him. His eyes met the intern's dark eyes, and he nodded. "Thank you."

"Thank you for your service, Mason. Please get help so you can help others. And I'm always here to talk with you if you want or need."

The intern left the room as quietly as he entered, and Mason hoisted himself up off the cold bench. He waited until his body adjusted to standing and his head stopped swirling. As soon as he was able, he shuffled to the Chief of Staff's office and knocked on the door. He couldn't be responsible for another life to be lost. He couldn't let the ghosts in the night increase in numbers. He needed to move on.

.   .   .

Thank you for reading **Seductive Nights** and this introduction to Mason Thompson from **Sensual Nights.** I hope this brief snippet of Mason has piqued your interest in **Sensual Nights.**

Mason thought he left the battlefield behind, but his past still haunts him. Now working as a bartender in Blossom Springs, he meets Carley Peters, a real estate agent rebuilding her life after a painful breakup. When Carley uncovers a dangerous secret in one of the condos she's selling, her life is thrown into peril.

As sparks ignite between them, Carley's life is threatened, and Mason must face his deepest fears to save her. Will love be enough to conquer the danger ahead?

To read more about who Carley and Mason are and how they get to Blossom Springs, jump into my newsletter group here – https://geni.us/SeductiveNightsBonusEp

Or - get your copy of *Sensual Nights* here.

https://geni.us/SensualEBPJF

ALSO BY PJ FIALA

I'm fortunate to be able to do what I love. It's a blessing.

My list of written works has gotten so long I needed to move it to my website! How's that for blessed?

Anyway, click the link below to see the list of all of my books.

Thank you so much for reading.

Click here to see a list of all of my books with the blurbs.

If you're reading a paperback, go to -

https://www.pjfiala.com/bibliography-pj-fiala/

MEET PJ

Writing has been a desire my whole life. Once I found the courage to write, life changed for me in the most profound way. Bringing stories to readers that I'd enjoy reading and creating characters that are flawed, but lovable is such a joy.

When not writing, I'm with my family doing something fun. My husband, Gene, and I are bikers and enjoy riding to new locations, meeting new people and generally enjoying this fabulous country we live in.

I come from a family of veterans. My grandfather, father, brother, two sons, and one daughter-in-law are all veterans. Needless to say, I am proud to be an American and proud of the service my amazing family has given.

My online home is https://www.pjfiala.com.
You can connect with me on
Facebook: https://www.facebook.com/PJFialaAuthor
Instagram: https://www.Instagram.com/PJFiala.
YouTube: https://youtube.com/@PJFiala
TikTok: https://www.tiktok.com/@pjfiala?lang=en
If you prefer to email, go ahead, I'll respond - pjfiala@ pjfiala.com.